Other Books Written by Neil Williams

For Adults

Irony
The Rabbit Died
Immigrant Tales
Short Stories
Too Many Deaths
Won't Stop 'til I Get Caught
Two for the Price of One
Too High
People are People Wherever You Go

For Children

The Rainbow Maker
Melissa and the Magic Whistle
Melissa and the Enchanted Island
Melissa and Her Scrap Book
The Red House
Herbert's Adventure

This is a story for

all the bad guys I know

Satch the Snatch

Written by

Neil Williams

A Short History

I was born into a family that didn't have much money. I had the same name as my father; Simon Atcheson. My father was a chronically, unemployed alcoholic and my mother was a drug addict, using anything she could find to get high. There was constant arguing and fighting in our household and when my father went to prison for some petty crime that he committed, my mother would bring men home, so that she could sell her body to make enough money to feed her various habits. She used very little of the money she made, to feed her children. We, always lived in very poor conditions, at home. Rats, lice, fleas, cockroaches and filth! My mother had a thing, against cleaning!

My father enjoyed punching and kicking me

when he came home drunk. I can't think of a time, going through my childhood when he wasn't doing that to me. I learned, that the best way to avoid most of the pain was to curl up into a fetal position and hold on tight! That helped! There came a point when I was about nine years old; both of my parents were in prison at the same time and my sister, Evelyn, 2 years younger than me, and I, were put into care. Over the years, we were in and out of care for long and short periods of time. When we weren't in care, we had to fend for ourselves, the best we could. I used to go into fruit and veg shops and quietly steal any food that I could. Sometimes I got caught and rather than being afraid at those times, it made me excited and I always had the urge to do it more! Some people, involved in the care of children do things to them that they shouldn't do. Withholding food, not having the heat turned on to save money, beatings and sometimes they do other things that make a child feel uncomfortable. My sister and I, experienced all of that and much more. We were separated, a couple of times and I always wondered, if I would see her again.

My sister, now, years after our childhood, is happily married and has two little ones of her own; a boy and a girl. I'm, Uncle Satch! Her husband is a hard working, honest guy and we get along. I wonder how she did that!

When I was about eight years old, the class had to check their scores on some tests that we had done. The marks were produced on a list, stuck to a bulletin board. We all went to see the list and we saw that everyone's name was listed as a letter, then the last name. Of course, my marks were crap! My name was listed as S. Atcheson. Two of my fellow students, Clarence and Arnold saw my name and after that they started to call me Satcheson. In a short time, it was changed to Satch and I've carried that name ever since. Everyone calls me Satch.

My impulse control problems started when I was six years old. I was very disruptive in school and after a school counselor spoke with me, they diagnosed me with a Conduct Disorder. Supposedly, impulse control disorders are over when a person reaches the age of 18. Mine has continued and now, at the age of 23, I am, as out of control as I always was!

At home, of course, it didn't matter what the disorder or ailment was; if it couldn't support a drug habit or supply money for cheap alcohol, it wasn't considered to be important. I drifted along, through a few different schools and, at least learned to read and write and do basic math.

The first signs of my disorder were made clear to everyone when I started to steal things in the classroom; things like blackboard erasers, chalk, books, pens and anything else I could get my hands on. I really enjoyed seeing the reactions of the people around me when they realised things were going missing. It was an absolute joy, to see the teacher or my fellow students looking high and low for something that I had taken and hidden. It made me laugh, hysterically! I had no use for those things and the reason I did it, was to see their reactions. I'm still the same way, today, which is why I'm in this trouble now! I would shout at the teachers, bully my fellow students and do whatever I could to cause the most disruption. The more the better!

As I got older, I started to shoplift and to run

past a woman and steal her handbag. I loved seeing how upset people got when I stole their things! It was a matter of survival now, so, I stole things to live. I was kicked out of the house when I was 14. My mother got a note from the school, telling her that if she couldn't get someone to treat my disorder, they would expel me from school. My mother's response was to kick me out! I said goodbye to my sister and lived on the street. No more school for me!

The Next Steps

When I was living on the street, I learned how to survive. There were other young people, like me, with similar backgrounds and we formed a family unit. Some kids were addicted to drugs and alcohol and had to sell their bodies to make money for their habit and, others, like me, were doing everything they could to keep living. Everyone looked out for everyone else! I stole purses, so people called me, Satch the Snatch. Actually, I like that name! It suits me!

As a person with a Conduct Disorder gets older, if untreated, it turns into an antisocial personality disorder and if it goes unchecked, as it did in my case, it begins to manifest itself, in very serious ways. The more stress I feel, the worse it is and, of course, I was experiencing stress, almost all the time! I would walk down the street and come across an elderly couple. I would, very quietly creep up on them and then scream in their ears as loudly as I could! The people of course, totally startled would almost faint from shock! I really liked that! I would run past a woman and scream and grab her purse! It really made me excited when I did that! I had no real friends and my condition didn't let me get close to anyone. I got arrested for shoplifting a couple of times when I was fifteen and got off with official bench warnings both times. No jail time.

One day, I had an idea. I was walking past a young woman with a small child, about 2 years old. She was holding the child's little hand and I wondered what she would do, if I ran up, picked up the child and ran off with it! I was sitting in Regent's Park, in London, watching them go by and as I watched them, all I could think about was how exciting it would be to take the child! I let them go by, but the idea wouldn't leave me! I continued to steal, to live and do purse snatching and a few break ins with some guys, I knew, but every time I sat on a park bench to watch the people go by, I would think about snatching a child.

One sunny day, I was sitting in Regent's Park, as usual and I decided that, today is the day to grab a little child. I wouldn't keep it, of course; I would let it go, after I saw the mother's reaction, which I expected would be amazing! I waited about an hour and then, there was a young, oriental woman, holding the hand of a very sweet looking, little girl, about two years old, wearing a little pink dress. As I watched them walk up to me, I thought of how my little sister had looked at that age and it made me smile. As they drew up to me, I stood, stretched and grabbed the child! I ran off, about 50 meters, put the child down and I stood, smiling with my hands on my hips. As I expected, the mother started to scream! And then, of course, the little one started to cry too! I was beside myself, I was so excited and happy! Look at the reaction I'd caused! I ran away, as people gathered around the mother and I watched from a distance, how things played out! Eventually, the police arrived and when they started to look for me, I made a quick exit! I knew every street and alleyway in the area, so I was never found.

Now, I had something to look forward to! I

used to lay in my cardboard box, near King's Cross Station, at night and laugh myself, silly, thinking about that mother and child's reaction! What a good thing! Now, I couldn't wait, until I could do it again!

A few days later, after I had stolen another purse, I was sitting in a different park, going through the contents of the purse, when I saw another mother and small child. The child was covered in a little flowered blanket and it was in a carriage. I could see that it wasn't belted in, the way most children are. It was very small. There were no other people around, so as they passed me, I jumped up, grabbed the child out of the carriage and ran off with it! The mother couldn't react to stop me and she started to scream, loudly! This time, I kept the child and kept running right out of the park, laughing my ass off! When I realised that I still had the child, I was far away from the park and I knew that I couldn't take it back, because, no doubt there would be a lot of people looking for it. Now, what do I do? Do I leave it here, on the street and walk away? Do I take it into a shop and leave it there? What? As I was walking along, I saw that the child had gone to sleep in my arms. It was calm and very light to carry.

I had a guy, a Scotsman, old Henry; an old thief and convict, that would fence credit cards and other things, I would find in purses. Now, I thought that the best thing to do with this little child, would be to take it to him and see if he wanted it. He had always said that he could fence anything that I would bring to him. He worked out of an old garage and when he saw me with the baby, he said, "And, what do ye have there, young Simon?"

I put the sleeping baby on his workbench and took out the things I'd found in the purse. I put them next to the baby and said, "Well, I've got these things from a purse, I got this morning."

He looked at the credit cards and ATM card, a nice leather wallet and a few small bits of jewelry and said, "Well, this ain't much. I'll give you £50 for the lot!" He crossed his arms over his chest, like he always did, expecting an argument and I, like I always did, started to pick the things up and he said, putting his hand on my arm, "OK, OK, then, ye bastard, I'll give you £65!"

I was used to this, so I smiled and said,

putting the things back on the bench, "Ah, yes, my old friend, now that's a much better price!"

He handed me the money and then he looked at the baby, "Are ye babysittin', today?"

I pretended that I didn't know what he meant, "Babysittin'?"

He poked the sleeping baby with his finger and said, "Yes, babysittin'!"

"Oh that, no, I stole that from the park!"

He looked surprised and said, "And what are ye gonna dae with it, now?"

I laughed and said, "I was kinda hoping, you could tell me that!"

He sat on a chair and smiled, "Do ye want to sell it, then?"

"Well, why not? I can't take it back without getting nabbed, so if you think you could find a buyer for it, then why not?"

He got out of the chair and went to the back of the garage, took out his mobile phone and dialed a number. I could hear him speaking but I couldn't hear his words. After a few minutes, he came back and said, "Right, I've spoken to someone and they're gonna come here and take a look at it. If they likes it, we're in for a big pay day! Could be as high as £5000!"

"£5000! Fuck mate, that's a lot of cash, ain't it?"

"Aye, laddie, that is a lot of cash! We'll split it, yes?" I nodded. He held out his hand for me to shake it; I did. Deal done!

Half an hour later, a big, black limo pulled in and a well dressed man and woman got out of it. The baby was awake, now and starting to squirm and cry a bit. The woman, dressed in a nice fur coat, came over, took the baby and went, with it, to the limo. She didn't look at me. The man took £5000 out of a briefcase and handed it to Henry. Not a word was spoken. The man went back to the limo, got in and it was gone! Less than one minute had passed and I, now had £2500 for doing, almost nothing! Henry handed me the money, laughed his sly laugh and said, "And that's how they do it, laddie!"

I took the money, looked at it and said, "Looks like we got a new business now, don't it!"

"That, we do, matey, that, we do!"

Police Business

The call came into the Anti Kidnap and Extortion Unit (AKEU) in the National Crime Agency at 13:30. DC George Mason took the call. George had been with the police for almost 25 years. He was balding, wore glasses and had a paunch that his wife called his Santa Claus Bulge. He listened for a moment and made a note in his notepad. He put the phone down and turned to his partner, DC Liz Dawson. "Child snatched from Green Park."

Liz stood up, "Right, let's go then." She had been with the police, in London for almost 15 years and she had been in the kidnap unit with George, as her partner for four years. She was blonde, short and had bright, blue eyes. She was always ready for action!

They drove to the park and found the usual

confusion. There were four constables and a very distraught woman, sitting on a bench next to an empty baby carriage. They showed their badges and went to speak with the woman. "Hello, ma'am, I'm DC Mason and this is my partner, DC Dawson. Can you tell us what happened?"

The woman was sobbing! "Some young guy just ran by and grabbed my little girl right out of the buggy! I tried to catch him but he was too fast! My poor little girl! She's gone!" She wailed!

George looked at his partner and shrugged. They'd heard this before. "Can you tell us what he looked like?"

"Yes, he was a young, white guy, slim, kind of wiry and he has long, light brown hair."

"What was he wearing?"

"Just a green T shirt and jeans, black trainers. Nothing unusual about him. He took my baby!" She burst into tears!

Liz said, "Where did he run to?"

The woman pointed, "Over there; he went out of the park towards the church."

George looked in the direction she had

pointed. He could see the CCTV cameras, nearby and he knew that they would have the guy recorded. There's almost nowhere in London that the cameras can't reach! "Can you tell us anything more, ma'am?"

She lowered her head and sobbed, "No, nothing else."

"Well, OK," George said, "please make sure that the officers have your contact details and we'll get on it right away. We should be able to find him and your baby. We'll do our best."

They walked away and George said, "We need to see the CCTV from those cameras over there."

There are an estimated 500,000 CCTV cameras in London, watching everything its citizens do. They went to the CCTV Monitoring Centre and were admitted by security. When they got to the monitoring room, they were met by Arnold Hastings, the centre manager. George knew him well, "Hello, Arnold, how are you, today?"

Arnold was a round, short man with spectacles and a big smile, "Oh, I'm OK, George. Hello Liz." He liked her. She smiled and nodded hello.

George said, "We're here on a kidnapping, Arnold. Baby taken from Green Park a few hours ago. Some young guy, grabbed it right out of its buggy! He ran in the direction of St. Margaret's Church."

Arnold sat at his desk and hit the keyboard. "A few hours ago? Can you be more specific?"

"Well, we got the call at 13:30, so it must have been a few minutes before then."

Arnold hit the keys, again and said, "OK, come here and see this." They went to look at his monitor and it showed Green Park, near where they had been talking to the distraught woman. A few minutes and they saw the woman, pushing the buggy with the baby in it and suddenly, a young guy wearing a green T shirt ran by and took the baby from the buggy! He was laughing, hysterically and he ran out of the park towards the camera. They had a very good look at his face! "Well, there he is." Liz said. She looked angry. "Brazen little fucker, isn't he!"

"Can we follow him, Arnold?" George asked.

Arnold hit the keys and another camera

showed the guy running with the baby, down a street and Arnold tried to get more cameras involved but after the third one, they had nothing. They could see where he was going but not his ultimate destination. "That's all we've got, I'm afraid," Arnold said.

"Well, it's something, at least. Thanks Arnold. I'd like to get close ups of his face from that camera, if possible."

"Yes, yes, of course. I'll have them sent over to you, before the end of the day."

"Good, we'll see you later."

They went back to their car. "Let's get up there and see if anyone saw this guy run by. Might be a chance, someone did," Liz said.

They drove to the last area covered by the camera and they spoke with a few of the locals but no one remembered seeing a guy with a baby. No surprise.

Making Money

Can you imagine me, with £2500 in my hand, all at one time! I walked out of Henry's place, not having any idea what I was going to do with all of that cash! The most I'd ever seen at one time, up to that point was about £150. I had nothing to do with drugs or alcohol and I slept in a cardboard box next to the wall of the train station. I crawled into my box, closed the flap and stared at the money! Of course, there were a lot of other people around, that, if they had seen the money, I wouldn't have been alive for very long! I held the money up to the little bit of light that was coming in. Now what? When you live on the street, money doesn't really matter. As long as you have enough to get you by, each day, it's usually enough.

I really didn't think, again, about the baby I

had stolen. If I thought of it at all, it was just to imagine, grabbing another one and selling it, too! I'm sure, there was a grieving family somewhere, but my personality disorder didn't allow me to have real feelings about it, one way or another. The thought of having another woman, screaming, so loudly, though, got me really excited!

The day after I got the money, I went to a different park and sat, eating a ham bagel and watching the people walk past. It was very early in the morning and not too many people were around; a few joggers and people walking their dogs. I wasn't, actually waiting for a new mother and child to pass by, but then I saw one. She was sitting on a bench, holding the baby by its little hands, so that it could stand up on her lap. It was a very young baby and very small, bouncing up and down and smiling at the woman. It was dressed in a little green dress, so I imagined it was a little girl. I didn't know it at the time, but later on, I found out that there is a market for babies to order. Skin colour, eye colour, race, religion, etc.

I, calmly finished my bagel and stood up. I

walked, slowly towards them, looked around and saw that there weren't any other people around and then I ran, grabbed the little baby and took off, out of the park as fast as I could run! The woman screamed and continued to scream very loudly! I was laughing, hysterically! The baby was almost weightless, it was so small! It wasn't making a sound, just looking around, confused. I wasn't far from Henry's, so I ran to his place and pounded on the door!

He was cautious when he opened it and when he saw the baby, he said, "Ah, well done, laddie! Get in here, now and I'll make the call!" I went inside and he called his contact.

A short time later, the same limo, with the same people arrived. The woman got out, again, not looking at me, took the baby and then the man paid Henry the money. This time, he said, "I will call you, soon, Henry. We have certain needs for some of our clients." He got into the limo and they were gone!

Henry peeled off £2500, smiled and said, "Now, that's real money, boy! Keep this up and we'll be rich men!"

I took the £2500 and stuck it in my shirt with

the rest. So far, I'd spent less than £5! I went to my box and crawled inside and lay there wondering what to do with it. I'd never had a real place to live, since I'd left home and I had no idea, how, to even find one. I had been living on the street for nine years, up to that point! All I had to my name was the clothes on my back, a few little trinkets, I'd kept from purses and my box!

There was a knock on the side of my box. When I opened it, Kylie, a girl, I knew was there, on her knees, trying to see into the box. She was small, had light pink hair and really light, almost green eyes. A real beauty! "Hey, what's up, babe?" I said.

"Hi Satch, can you help me out?"

She needed drugs, "Well, I don't know sweety. What'll ya give me for it?"

She licked her lips and said, "How about a nice, slow blow job?"

I laughed, because we'd had this same conversation lots of times! She knew, I'd never want her to do that, because I had too much respect for her and I was never really into sex! I reached into my pocket, took out a £20 note, threw it at her and said, "I wouldn't let that mouth, anywhere near my cock!"

"Well, fuck me; look who's rich! Looks like bein' a lowly purse snatcher pays off sometimes, don't it; Satch the Snatch!"

I stroked her cheek, smiled and said, "Take that money and fuck off, before I take it back!"

She smiled, reached out, and stroked my cock, stood up and said, "Any time you want it, baby, you know where my box is." She nodded at her box, next to mine, got up and walked away, slowly, emphasising her nice bum and went to buy some drugs.

Liz took the call this time. She listened and nodded and wrote in her notebook. "We've got another one, George. Same thing. A young guy stole a little baby from Wharf Road Gardens."

"Good CCTV around that area." He was holding the photo of the man in the green shirt. "Let's see if it's the same guy."

They went to the park and saw the crying mother. Same questions. Same guy, wearing a red T shirt this time. They went to see Arnold and yes, there he was. He did it, exactly the same way. He ran up, stole the child and ran out of the park, laughing. He was not trying to hide his identity. They followed him, as far as the cameras would allow and when he couldn't be followed any more, they went to look at a map. "Looks like he's going in the same direction as before.," Liz said. "Maybe he lives around there. What the Hell is he doing with the babies, though?"

"I guess we got a serial kidnapper on our hands, here, partner. Not a good thing. He's probably selling them."

"But, to whom?"

Orders Please

I didn't have a mobile phone, because, I actually didn't have anyone to call, so a few days later, I was sitting next to Regent's Canal when one of the guys I knew, Maurice, a pantomime specialist, came up to me and said, "Hey Satch, Henry called and asked me to find you. He said, he has somethin' for you at his place."

I stood up, "Oh, OK, then, I'll go and see him. Thanks, Mo."

I went to Henry's place and when I went inside, the guy from the limo was there, standing next to Henry. He was very well dressed, in a dark suit, blue tie and very nice, expensive shoes. He looked like some kind of foreigner and like he had a lot of money. "So, here ye are, finally, laddie!" Henry said.

"Do you not have a mobile phone, young man?" the guy asked.

I said, "No, I don't. I don't have anyone to call!"

He reached into his coat and brought out a small, burner phone, "This will be your phone. We will call you on it when we have an new order."

I took the phone but I had no idea what he meant by 'order'. "Order?"

He smiled, "Yes, we get orders for certain characteristics and we, sometimes will need you to find a baby with those. It is worth a lot more money when you can do it, so it is worth your while to work with us."

I looked at Henry. He said, "Well, Guzim, we will certainly do what we can to assist you." Posh asshole!

"Where do you live?" the man asked me.

"I live in a very nice, cardboard box, next to King's Cross Station."

"A cardboard box?" I nodded. "Well, surely you have enough money, now to find a nice apartment, no?" He had some kind of foreign accent.

I couldn't place it. I'd have to ask Henry about this guy. "I will have my colleague find you a suitable place and then you can sleep a bit more comfortably. Would you like that?"

"Um, I guess so. I've never had a place, so I guess it'll be different, at least."

"Good, well, don't worry about the rent. We will pay that for you. You work for us, now, so we will take care of you."

I wasn't sure, how I felt about working for this guy or anyone, as I'd never worked for anyone in my life but I thought that I might as well see where it goes. I held up the phone, "OK, sounds good."

"Yes, she will call you later, today. We have a number of houses and flats around the country and you will stay in one of those. We find it best, if you take the babies from different parts of the country to avoid the police catching you, so we will make sure that your travel costs are covered also. All you have to do is wait for the call. We will tell you, exactly what to bring us and when you do it, you will be more than compensated for your efforts. You will not be given, anyone's names and, aside from my colleague calling you about the flat, I will be your only contact. We keep some girls in houses around the country, so if you can find any that we can use, that will add to your income. The younger the better. We also use children in pornographic films, so we are always looking for new ones, there, also. You are good at getting babies, so keep those things in mind. Small children are just as easy to obtain."

Now, I was getting nervous! Who the fuck is this guy? I'd known a few girls that had disappeared from the streets, over the years! Now, I was thinking, that this was probably one of the people responsible for that! Him and his so called colleague! What am I getting into, here?

He stood up, "OK, Henry, you will, of course still get your share of the funds as a commission but we will, in future, deal, directly, with this young man." He looked at me, "And what is your name?"

"My name is Satch."

"Satch, well, good, wait for our call, later, today." He went out, without looking back.

"What the fuck, Henry?"

He laughed, "What do ye mean, laddie?"

"What the fuck do I mean? Who is this guy?"

"Oh, ye dinna want to know that, matey! Him and his people are what ye call, mobsters! Real villains! They got operations all over Europe and they ain't to be fucked with; that's certain! They's Albanians! Them houses for girls he talked about, also have young men, like you, chained to a bed, suckin' cocks and gettin' buggered all day. There are some there, that thought they could take advantage of these people and now they's bein' punished! And that colleague of his, as he called her, is the one that's runnin' the show! It ain't him! He's, just her yes man! It'll be a few babies here and there and ye'll live well, for as long as ye wants to! They'll pay for young girls and kids, so see what ye can do there, as well."

I sat on a chair and put the phone in my pocket. 'Right, I'm in it, now!'

He nodded, "Aye, ye are that! Well done, you!"

My New Job

I stayed with Henry, for just a few more minutes, then I left him without saying goodbye. I wanted to think. I imagined that I could, just throw the phone away, take the £5000 and fuck off! I was rich, so I could do anything! Of course, my disorder would never let me think, like that, rationally, for very long. As I walked back to my box, I saw four school girls in their uniforms, waiting for a bus and I couldn't stop myself from screaming at them as I went past them! When they screamed, I laughed, and pretended to be a wild animal! I pounded on a car window and spat in the face of the driver, an old lady! The window was closed but the look of disgust on her face, started me laughing again

When I got near my box, I was hungry, so I went to a kiosk and bought a sandwich. I'd been, so used to scraping around and having no food, most of the time, that I never thought of going to sit in a restaurant and having an actual meal. The thought never crossed my mind! I knew that I would act up in a restaurant, anyway, so I didn't go into them. People don't like it, when someone is screaming at them or pissing on the floor when they're trying to eat. I had done that a couple of times and even though it gave me a good laugh to see my piss running down the floor, I felt I needed to control myself today. I was waiting for a phone call.

I went to my usual place next to the canal and started to eat my sandwich. The phone rang, "Hello?"

It was a woman. Same accent as the guy, "Go to the address, I will text you in the next minute. The keys will be in the shop and your new place is on the first floor." She hung up and a few seconds later, I got a text message with an address.

I knew the area. It was a long row shops on the high road and it had flats above it, not far from Brixton Tube Station. I finished my sandwich and walked over there. When I went into the shop, the guy said, "Satch?" Same accent.

"Yeah, that's me."

He handed me some keys, "The blue door next to us. Apartment two." He turned his back on me.

I took the keys from him and went outside. I opened the blue door with the key and went up the stairs to a landing and saw, apartment number two on my left. It was a small, one bedroom place, with a living room, with a single bed in it, a separate kitchen with a fridge and cooker, a bathroom and a few pieces of cheap furniture. I opened the cupboards and found basics, like cups, plates, pots and pans and utensils. Nothing special. I went into the bathroom and saw that there were two towels. I stripped off my clothes and had a warm shower for the first time in three weeks! I let the bath fill up and laid in the water, thinking, for almost two hours! Luxury! When you live in a box, you never have such a pleasant experience!

As I lay in the bath, I could hear people, entering and leaving the apartment across the hall. It sounded like the door opened and closed a lot.

Probably one of their places with the girls and kids. Later, I was proved to be right. They had six girls and a few kids for rent over there. More of that, later.

After my bath, I sat on the sofa, wondering what to do. I had more money than I'd ever had in my life, so I didn't need to do any shoplifting or purse snatching and I kind of felt like I would miss that. Other than needing money to survive, I liked to grab purses, so I could see the reaction of the women I was robbing. I looked around the room. I'd need a TV. I'd never owned one and when I looked at the wardrobe, I realised I didn't have any clothes, either. Time to do some shopping!

I went downstairs, into the street and stood there, wondering how to buy clothes. In all the time I'd lived on the street, I'd always gotten my clothes and shoes, free, from charities. I saw a charity shop across the street, selling used clothes, so I went into it. There were racks of all kinds of clothes, so I looked them over and bought three shirts and some jeans and a nice pair of black trainers. When the woman said, £12 for everything, I couldn't believe it was that cheap! I handed her a 20 and she smiled and gave me the change.

I went back to the apartment and changed my clothes. I looked at myself in the mirror and smiled. I was wearing used jeans and a yellow polo shirt. It, actually had a collar on it! I saw a young, slim, healthy guy, not too tall with long, light brown hair and blue eyes, looking back at me. I turned this way and that and smiled at myself. I saw that I needed a shave. It had been a long time, since I'd spent any time looking at myself in a mirror! I laughed loudly! "You look good, kid!"

I went to a diner down the street and had a nice, thick, ham and cheese omelet with chips and lots of tea and didn't even think of pissing on the floor! I was sitting, quietly, looking out at the people passing by when the mobile rang, "Hello?"

The woman, "We need a young, Indian boy baby. Same age, as the girl, the other day. Bring it to Henry when you have it." The phone went dead. 'Like she was orderin' a fuckin' pizza'! I thought. I sat, looking at the dead phone and shook my head! I paid for my meal and left the diner.

As I walked down the street, I realised it was a sunny day and that, probably my friends would be looking for me. I went to my box and sure enough, there was Kylie, sitting outside it, waiting for me, "Well, well, here comes the fucking purse snatcher and wearing new clothes! Where have you been Satch?"

I sat next to her, put my arm around her and said, "Now, listen, babe, I got somethin' to tell you, that's important. I got an apartment now." She turned to look at me. I continued, "I'm into to some really, serious shit!" I took a wad of cash, about £500, out of my shirt and handed it to her.

She wouldn't take it! "No, no, Satch, you ain't givin' that money to me! Too much! Whatever you're doin' to get this, you'd better stop, right now! Nothin' good'll come of it! I don't know who gave it to you and I don't wanna know what it is, but," she looked at the money, "whatever it is, get out now!" She stood up, frowned, waved her finger at me and walked away. She wasn't moving her ass the same way, today. She didn't look back!

I sat there for a while. I'd known Kylie for

almost two years and for most of that time, we had had our boxes close to each other. We'd spent hours, sitting together, talking about how our lives were, how we'd gotten there and when and if, it would ever get better. She was a really good girl, in spite of her heroin addiction. She'd been sexually abused, for years by her father and her brother and she'd finally run away from Manchester when she was 12, to come to live on the streets in London. She was a really tough, street smart girl! She was 17 now and sold herself and did whatever she could to get high, every day, just like my mother and so many kids that have grown up on the streets. More than 10,000 people are homeless in London and almost all of them have a similar story to tell. A lot of them, like me, have mental health problems and are substance abusers. Social services in the UK is broken and these are the people that fall through the cracks. Very few people, especially in government, care about them!

But, I had to find a little, Indian baby! Where would I go, to get one of those? It was midday and I sat there, thinking about it. London, is informally divided up along ethnic lines. Some areas have a lot of Muslims or Greeks or Cypriots or Chinese and other nationalities. Southhall, on the far west side of London, is known as one of the largest Indian areas. The problem was, that I could easily snatch a baby, but then I'd be far away from Henry's place and I'd have to cross, almost the whole city to get back here. I'm not the smartest or most logical guy in existence and I'd never had to, really do much serious thinking about anything. I was and am, all about impulse! See something, do it, laugh like Hell and then go and do something else, outrageous! I'd been doing that my whole life.

As I sat there, I saw a delivery guy with a red bike, with a carrier on the front, go into a shop carrying a big box and then I had an idea; steal the bike, cycle across London, grab a baby and stick it in the carrier! I got up, walked very calmly to the bike, sat on it and peddled away. As I turned the corner, I could hear the delivery guy, yelling that someone had stolen his bike! I couldn't stop myself from howling with laughter! I peddled, as fast as I could and then headed to Southhall. It took me about an hour and as I went into it, I could see, Indians of all shapes and sizes, walking in and out of the many, Indian shops.

There are three parks in Southhall; Jubilee Park, Southhall Park and Three Bridges Park. I didn't know the area, really well but I'd been there a few times with a couple of people and with Kylie when she was looking for drugs. We used to go there to beg for money, sometimes. Indians can be quite generous. I went into Southhall Park and sat on a bench and looked around. There were too many people and I was the only non Indian, there! No one paid, obvious, attention to me but I knew that people would be watching me. As the people went by, I saw a couple of likely targets but then it came to me; how the fuck do I know, if it's a boy or a girl, baby! At that age, they could be wearing anything! I was on the edge of letting out a loud scream, so I got up and went to the next park!

As I walked through the park, pushing the bike, I saw a young Indian woman in a sari, changing a baby's diaper. A boy! He was just the right size and age! I sat on a bench and waited for her to finish changing it. She got up, put the baby in a buggy, without strapping it in and then a large, Indian guy wearing a bright green turban, came over to her and started to talk to her. The father? She stopped walking and I could hear that they were talking in a language, I didn't understand. The guy reached into the buggy and picked up the baby. He smiled, said something to the woman, put it back in the buggy and then he walked away! Good, not the father as I had thought! Now, I really wanted to scream, I was so excited! She walked through the park, pushing the buggy and stopping to chat to people from time to time and then she went to the exit. I got up, walked very slowly, pushing the bike and I followed her, keeping a good distance between us. She turned onto a quiet street with normal, small houses. I put the bike against a fence and walked, quickly up to her! I tapped her on the left shoulder and when she turned to see who had touched her, I went onto her other side and grabbed the little baby! She didn't have time to react, except to scream, which started me laughing, because that was what I'd been hoping for and then I sprinted back to the bike, threw the baby into the carrier and I was off! I was peddling as fast as possible and unlike my part of London, I didn't know the area at all! I cycled down the street and then I went back towards London as fast as I could go. Now, the baby started to cry! Fuck, now what?

I stopped, next to a small shop and went in and bought some milk. Of course, I know fuck all about babies and what they need! I opened the milk, poured some onto my fingers and dripped it into the baby's mouth! After a few tries, the baby started to lick the milk off of my fingers and in a short time, it was calmer. I got back on the bike and peddled it, all the way to Henry's place. I was sweating like Hell! When I knocked on the door, he opened it, looked in the carrier and said, "Well done, laddie! They told me, ye'd be by with one of these today!" He picked up the baby, looked at it and said, "Indian, all right! Here comes the real money, now, son!" He went to make the phone call. I heard him laughing into the phone and then he came back to me and said, "Now, that's a very happy man, laddie! Ten grand this time! That's seven thousand for you and three thousand for me!"

"Seven thousand for me?"

He nodded and smiled, "Aye, that's the new split, alright! You're gettin' 70%! Did ye no ken that?"

I shook my head, "No, I never even thought about it!"

"Aye, well that's how it's gonna be from now on, matey! 70% for you! If ye can manage to do a couple o' these a month, ye'll be a very rich man, very soon!

The limo arrived. The same man and woman got out of it and when the woman came over, this time, she looked at me, nodded and took off the baby's diaper. She looked at its penis, smiled and looked at the man and nodded. He took the cash out of his briefcase, gave me, £7000 and £3000 to Henry. Not a word was spoken, until the man was getting back into the limo. "We'll call you soon, Satch." He smiled and got into the car beside the smiling woman! Two minutes, tops!

"Southhall this time." George said.

"Yes," Liz said, "we should be able to track him right across the city. Let's get Arnold on it, right away. If he comes back to the same area, maybe we can narrow his destination down." She called Arnold and told him what they needed. They went to the CCTV Centre and he was waiting for them.

"I've managed to track him, right across the city. He's on a red push bike. Watch this." He hit the keys and the scene appeared. They could see the different camera numbers and they could also see how crazy he looked as he rode the bike. They watched him stop at the shop and give the milk to the baby and then, they saw him riding the bike past King's Cross and around a corner and then he was gone.

"Nothing more, I'm afraid, after that. We have no cameras in that area."

Liz looked at George. "He looks deranged doesn't he!"

George nodded, "Yes, he certainly does. Different clothes and shoes though. Maybe he bought them locally."

Liz smiled at Arnold, "Thanks Arnold. We'll let you know how we get on." Arnold smiled and nodded. He rarely spoke to Liz!

The Employers

"You sure this boy is going to be OK, Guzim?"

"Yes, Flutura. I have had him checked out and although he is homeless, he is clean; no drugs, no alcohol and look what he has done, so far. I think we can rely on him." She was tall, slim, well dressed and coiffed; her dark hair was piled high on her head and she was manicured and lived a life of luxury. In her early forties, she knew that she could stay in the business for many more years. Her fingers sparkled with diamonds! Nothing was too good for her!

"If anything goes wrong, it will be on both of us, you know that."

Guzim smiled; inwardly he was terrified of this woman but he could never let it show. He knew that she was a ruthless murderer and she would think nothing of having him killed. In fact, he knew that she would enjoy watching it happen! She had no loyalty to anyone but their leader, Bardhyll Gega, back home in Albania,. He was their chief and he and his family had been in the business, since before time began. They had every type of illegal activity that could exist, including gambling and drug dealing. Their biggest business was people trafficking in all its forms. Guzim knew that they had thousands of people in their control, all over the world, working as prostitutes, slaves in homes and factories and they made a fortune on child and other types of pornography. They got as much as £100,000 for some of the babies that were brought to them. The Russians worked with them and their connections in the Middle East for enslaved women was the best in the world. They took hundreds of women and children from places like Vietnam, the Philippines, Africa and Cambodia. Their connection with the Mexican and Latin American cartels was better than anyone else on earth! They did huge business with organised crime in Brazil, America and Canada. The trade in humans, globally, involves, every type and age of person and is worth billions. It is carried out, in almost every country on earth and his employers were there, leading the world!

It was said, that their employers went back to the days of the African slave trade! Not the kind of people to get on the wrong side of! He had been in business with them, since he was a young teenager back home in Tirana, the capital of Albania and he and his family were part of their family.

He and Flutura had the responsibility of all business in the UK. She had been born into the business, so for her, kidnapping and selling babies, children and young men and women, came as second nature. He had discussed it with her and she had told him that the people meant nothing to her. She had no husband, no boyfriend and she had said that she was married to the business. He knew that she used some of the young men and women for sex but she had always said, that it just like scratching an itch for her! He really was afraid of her!

The Neighbours

I looked at the money and then I looked at Henry. "Is this what they call, the big time, Henry?"

He shook the cash in his hand, "I guess it is, laddie. I've never been into anythin' like this, in all my years, that's certain! I canny believe it, actually."

I looked, right into his eyes, "It's fuckin' dangerous though, ain't it!"

"Dangerous! Dangerous on all sides, mate! The cops'll be on this, sure and these people in the limo, ain't to be fucked with! As I told ye, if ye fuck it up, the penalty'll, be, you chained to a bed with cocks bein' stuck in you all day! Me, they'll just drop me in the Thames with a big knife in me back! Aye, it's fuckin' dangerous, alright! I got a way out, though, do you?"

"A way out?"

"Aye, a way out. I got a wee place and I'm no gonna say where, but it's in Europe, in the sun. I'm no gonna tell ye more than that, in case you gets tortured! The less ye knows, the better!"

"What the fuck do you mean, tortured?"

"These are Albanians, mate! Kosovo, all that! Do ye know ken it?"

I shrugged, "I've never heard of Kosovo!"

Henry shook his head, "Well, just let me tell ye, laddie; these is the worst of the worst! They's doin' people traffickin', on a large scale, all over the world! They works with the Russians, the Sicilians, the Chinese, the Thais and Vietnamese and them Arabs in Dubai! This is big time shite, that's for sure! You gets on their wrong side and ye'll be lucky, if all ye gets is torture! However, if ye works with 'em, they'll make ye a very rich man! Ye'll have anything ye wants, that's sure! That baby, there'll, probably sell for a hundred grand in their market. They sells them for their organs and really rich people buys 'em 'cause they can't have kids! They wants, them young girls, too, so that they'll work as sex slaves! Lotsa men likes the young, white girls. Places like Japan,

Saudi and China'll pay big money for 'em, aye! This is real big business!" He smiled at me and nodded at the money. "So, what're gonna do wi' all that candy, there?"

"I, actually don't have a fuckin' clue, mate! I've never had more than a few rags and a cardboard box, so I got no idea what to do with it. They gave me a small flat, that, actually has a bath tub and I bought a few clothes but I got no idea what to do with it all! I tried to give some of it to my friend but she almost ran away when she saw it!"

He put his hand on my arm, "Hey, hey, mate, be careful! Dinna be showin' that cash to naebody! Keep yer freends safe and leave them alone. Just go and tell them that yer goin' to Europe or anywhere and then leave them alone. Better for them, that's for sure. You homeless people are always disappearin', so no one'll miss ye, that's sure! What they dinna know, they canny tell the Bill, if they're asked, innit? The Bill'll be all ower the place, soon and the more you keep a low profile, the better. The last thing you want, is for they Albanians to know that you've got pinched, so be very careful, alright?

Ye'll no be safe in prison! I had an Albanian cellmate, a rapist, for 4 months in Pentonville, so I knows how dangerous they are! There's a lot o' 'em in there and it'll be nothin' for 'em to close yer yap if they think yer gonna open it!"

I shoved the cash into my shirt and said, "You can sell this bike if you want; I don't need it." I left him.

I went to my box and sat in front of it. A few minutes later, Kylie came over, "You gonna take my advice?"

"Advice?"

She punched my shoulder! "Advice, you fuckin' idiot!" She punched my stomach and felt the money inside my shirt! "You see! Take that fuckin' money and throw it in the Thames or burn it! Get inside your box and forget the people that gave it to you! You're probably, already too late but get out while the gettin's good before you get in too far!" I started to speak and she put her fingers over my mouth, "No, Satch, don't say anything! I've known you, here in this box for over a year and I know, that aside from bein' a thief, you don't do much of anything else, unlike some of these assholes around here, so don't get into somethin' that's worth all this money! You're gonna get hurt real bad, if you do!"

I should have listened to her!

She took her fingers off of my lips and I said, "OK, I came here to tell you, to tell, everyone that I'll be going away from here. I can't tell you where I'm going but you might start to see some cops around here, soon and you don't know where I am." I kissed her cheek and said, "Now, how much money do you want? I got tons of it!"

She kissed me on the lips and stood up, "I'm really gonna miss you, baby! Give me £20, like you always do and I'll go and see my friend, OK? I don't want more than that."

I handed her a £50 note and she looked at it and waved her finger in my face, "Too much, boy, way too much!" She walked away, shaking her head. She looked worried.

I waited, until she went around the corner, then I took out a handful of cash, went to her box and tucked it under her pillow. I walked, slowly back to my apartment and when I got to the shop, I bought some eggs, bread, milk, coffee and some colas and went up to my flat. I used to make fried eggs for me and Evelyn when we were kids and now that I had somewhere to cook, I wanted some of that. As I was opening the door, the door behind me opened. A dark haired, fat woman was standing there. She looked me up and down and said, "Who the fuck are you? You want some young pussy, yes?"

I wanted to smash her face in! I looked her up and down, the way she'd looked at me and I said, "I'm your new neighbour. My name is Satch and you don't want me to get upset with you, so get back inside and make sure that you leave me, alone, OK? I'm not interested in young pussy or anything else you have to offer, got it?"

A very large, dark haired man, with a big paunch, in a dirty undershirt, came up behind her and smiled at me, "Hello Satch, I am Gjin. I know, you're an OK guy; I was told!" Same accent. "Sasha, here, don't know about you, yet, so please, let's be calm, alright?" Downstairs, the blue door opened and a man came up the stairs. "Ah, Malcolm, you're here! Lily is already wet, waiting for you! Please go in! She is on the bed, ready for you. Come in, my friend!" He turned to me, "We will see you, later, Satch! Come Sasha, let's make sure Malcolm gets what he needs. Make sure he has the whip he wants." He smiled at me and closed the door.

I went into the flat and sat on the sofa. I looked around the room and realised that I didn't even have a radio to listen to! I knew of a shop, not far away, called Bill's Boxes, where they sold TVs and stereo equipment. I walked over there and went inside. I saw a very nice, large, flat screen TV. The sign said, 40" UHC 3D TV. £699.

A salesman came over and looked me over, "Hello, sir, how may be of service today."

"I'll have this TV. Can you have it delivered today? I live close by."

He nodded, "And how will you be paying for this, sir?" He looked unsure, probably thinking I didn't have any money.

I went to the other side of the room and looked at the stereos. Big speakers, amplifier, DVD player. The sign said, surround sound. £599. "Can this be hooked up to my TV?"

He nodded, "Yes, of course, sir and how will you be paying for this?" Still unsure.

"Will it be installed at this price?"

"Yes, of course, sir."

I took out a roll of £50 notes and counted out £1300. I added an extra £50 and said, writing down the address, "Today, yes?"

He was all smiles now! He looked at the address, "Yes, sir, within the hour, sir!" A happy man!

I went back to the flat, fried two eggs and made some toast. I made a coffee and as I was finishing it, there was a knock on the door. I opened it and there were two big guys standing there. "We got a TV and stereo for you, mate."

"Ah, good, great, bring it in here!"

They carried in the boxes and in half an hour, they had it all hooked up and working. I gave, each of them, £20 and they were happy when they went out. I sat on the sofa, picked up the remote and found a channel showing music videos. I turned the sound up, high, on my new stereo and then I howled like a wolf! Look at this rich fucker!

I guess, I must have fallen asleep because I suddenly jerked awake! Someone was knocking on my door! I turned down the music and opened the door and Gjin was there, smiling, "So, my friend, it looks like you got a new TV, huh?"

"Yeah, I did, Gjin. What can I do for you?"

"Well, we are having a party tonight and I would like you to attend."

"A party?"

"Yes, yes, we have a party, every weekend and this is Saturday!"

"What time will it be happening?"

"About 8:00, we will get started but it will go on all night, so you are welcome, any time. We have some nice girls and young women here, so you may enjoy yourself, if you join us."

"Well, OK, Gjin, thanks for telling me. I might be there."

I closed the door and sat on the sofa. I watched TV for a while and then I went to get some chicken. When I came back, I could hear the music from inside the other flat; the party had started.

I finished my food and then I went next door.

I knocked on the door and it was opened by a girl about 12 years old. She was wearing a see through top and panties. "Hello, I'm Lily," she said, smiling at me. She sounded French. I could see the bruises on her body. She opened the door wider and said, "You're Satch, aren't you?" I nodded. "Well, come in, Satch, Gjin is waiting for you."

I went inside and there were five men and I could see two women, about 20 years old and Lily with three other young girls, the same age as her. They were, all, almost naked.

Gjin saw me, "Ah, so you are here, my young friend! Good to see you! Come to me, Minh!" he said to one of the girls. She was about 20 years old. She came over and I could see that she looked Japanese or maybe Vietnamese. She was wearing a light blue, see through top and very small panties that barely covered her ass. She smiled at me. "Give him some head, my girl! He will like that!" She got on her knees and reached for my zip.

I pushed her hand away and pulled her to her feet. "I'm takin' this one over to my place, Gjin." I smiled at him.

58

"Yes, nice idea, my boy! Take her away with you!"

I pulled Minh out the door and into my flat. She came along, calmly. I sat her on the sofa and she started to take off her panties. "Stop, Minh," I said.

She looked confused, "You don't want to fuck me?"

I sat beside her and took her hand, "No, babe, I don't want to fuck you and I don't want a blow job."

"So, what do you want?" She looked scared.

"I want you to sit here with me, have a cola and watch TV."

"You must be fuckin' crazy man! I cannot do that!"

I laughed, "You cannot do it? Why not?"

She looked surprised, "Because I am a cunt for anyone to use! If you do not want me, then I have to go back and find someone else! I cannot stay here, if you do not fuck me!" She tried to stand up.

"But, why can't you stay here?"

"Because, if Sasha or Gjin ever found out, they will beat me and maybe hurt my family back home! I cannot stay here, if you do not want to fuck me!" She tried to get up, again.

I held her back and went and locked the door, "Now, here's what you're gonna do," I said. "I'm going into the kitchen and here's the remote." I handed her the remote. "I want you to find us a good film and we're gonna sit here and drink colas and watch a film. We're not gonna fuck and you can stay here as long as you want. Sasha and Gjin'll never find out and all we're gonna do, is sit here and relax. Do you want something to eat?" She nodded, warily. "Do you like fried eggs on toast?" I didn't know how to cook anything else! She nodded, again. "Good, I'll make us, some nice, fried egg sandwiches and we can watch a film; now, see if you can find one for us." I took a blanket off of the bed and covered her with it. Finally, she smiled.

While I was in the kitchen making the eggs, I could hear her changing channels. I made two egg sandwiches, each, for us and took them to her. She ate like she was starving and she put her hand on my shoulder and said, "Thank you, so much, Satch. I will never forget this!" We watched three films, drank all of the cola and then we went to bed. We cuddled and she wanted me to fuck her but I told her, that all she had to do was go to sleep. "I just want to thank you," she said.

"Well, thank me, by letting me cuddle you, until we fall asleep, OK?" She put her arms around me and we went to sleep.

More Orders

When I woke up in the morning, I was next to a very sweet smelling, naked, young woman! This was a first for me. Although I had had sex with a few women, it was usually in my box with hard cement under us. I'd never, actually had a woman in bed with me. I put my arms around her and kissed her neck. She woke up and said, "So, we fuck now?"

I laughed and said, "Do you want to fuck me because you have to or do you want to fuck me?"

She took my cock in her hand and said, "I am horny for the first time, in a long time and I really want to fuck you!" We had sex and it was great!

We took a shower together, her squealing and me laughing and then we finished the eggs and the bread. While we were eating, I asked, "So, what about you, Minh?"

"About me?"

"Yes, about you? How came you here?"

"Oh, well, they took me from my home, in Saigon when I was 14 years old and they have moved me, every few months to different houses, in different countries, so that I can have sex with many, many men! I am now 19 years old and they keep promising to let me go, but I know they never will! I cannot escape and if I try, they will kill my family in Vietnam! I am a prisoner!"

I felt sorry for her. Someone knocked on the door! Gjin! "So, you greedy man! You keep my best girl, all night?! He looked at Minh, frowned, almost snarled and pointed at their door. She jumped to her feet and ran out of the room, naked, without looking back! She was afraid! "Now, my friend, you will get a phone call today. I will see you later!" He went into his flat and I heard him yelling at Minh, saying her name over and over!

An hour later, the phone rang. "Hello?"

Her. "Another young one, white with blue eyes this time. A boy but if it is a girl, it is OK. Bring it to Henry, as usual." She hung up.

Fuck! I could feel the excitement starting to rise in me! I couldn't wait to see the mother's face and hear her scream! The sex with Minh had been good, but to hear the anguished scream of the mother when I grabbed her child, aroused me, just as much! I really, really loved to hear that! Nothing could beat it!

Now, where to find a blue eyed, blonde haired baby? Obviously one of the parks, but wouldn't the police be watching for that in London? Richmond Park; outside of London; lots of people go there for walks but like Southhall, it was far away, so why not closer? The place where I had my box was always crowded with tourists. There were a lot of small hotels, nearby and lots of families used them. Maybe, I could follow a mother to one of those and grab the kid?

I got dressed in my new clothes and took the bus to where I had my box. I'm very street wise, after so many years living in the street and I've snatched hundreds of purses, so I know how to watch a crowd. I saw a few good possibilities but none of them were going where I needed them.

Finally, I saw a young woman pushing a buggy with a baby inside. I walked towards them and yes, the baby had blue eyes and blonde, curly hair. Looked like a boy; it was wearing a little blue outfit. I passed them and then turned to follow them. I was so excited, I was vibrating! She went into one of the hotels and into the lift. I followed her in and watched the dial, showing the floors and saw that she got off on the fifth floor. It was a small, hotel, so I imagined that there were, only three or four rooms per floor. I looked around, to be sure that no one saw me and I took the stairs, two at a time to the fifth floor. There were four doors. I stood in front of each one and listened. The first one had a man inside; I heard him speaking to someone. The next one was quiet, probably empty and the third one was it! I heard the woman talking, like you would speak to a baby and then I waited, listening to see if there was a man's voice. Her mobile rang! "Yes," I heard her say, "Jeff is still out with William. He'll be here in about an hour."

I waited until she closed the phone, then I knocked on the door. When she opened it, she said,

"Yes?" I was so excited, I could hardly stop myself from screaming! This was grabbing fifty purses at the same time! I pushed her into the room, shut the door before she could say anything, then I punched her on the chin! She went down onto the bed, unconscious and then I saw the sleeping baby! I fell onto the bed beside her, put my face into the pillow and screamed, three times, as loud as I could! I picked up the baby with its little, yellow blanket and went out of the room. It was sound asleep and didn't notice that I had picked it up. Down the stairs, look around the hotel lobby and out the door. I went straight to Henry's place and knocked on the door.

"Oh, ye little fucker!" he said, laughing. "That were quick, weren't it! Come in, now, get in here!" He looked at the sleeping baby and said, "My, my, ye gots a way with them little uns don't ye!" He made a phone call and within twenty minutes, the limo arrived. She got out, took the baby, nodded at me and he handed us the money. One minute and they and the baby were gone!

Task Force

"He used violence this time. Brazen son of a bitch! Right under the cameras! Same guy, dressed the same way! He looks like, he thinks he won't get caught!"

Liz smiled, "So far, he's right! Look at him!" They were watching the video for the fifth time!

"Well, we've run his face though our system and no matches. It looks like he's never been arrested."

"We need to speak with the chief, George; get a task force going on this one."

George ran his hand over his face. He always did that when he experienced stress. "OK, I'll go and see him. We've done all we can do, alone on it. We need help, for sure."

George went up to see his boss, Detective Chief Inspector (DCI), Jim Morgan. He knocked on the door of the office. "Come in."

"Hello Jim, how are you today?"

"I'm good, George, very good. How about you?"

"I'm good. Got a little problem, though."

Jim sat back in his chair, indicating the chair in front of his desk for George to sit in. George sat. "So, what's the problem?"

"Well, we, me and Liz have been trying to catch this baby stealer that's been taking the babies from our parks. We've spent a lot of time looking at the CCTV and we know what he looks like but so far nothing. We can, always track him to a certain point and then he's gone. We've interviewed, along with the boys from the Met (Metropolitan Police), a lot of people but no one has seen the guy. We're sure he's not going to stop, so we want to set up a task force that can assist us."

"A task force, you say?" George nodded. "How many men?"

"I think, three to start with, then we can canvass, a lot more distance and maybe get a hit."

"Well, we don't have a lot of people that can

be free to do it, you know."

"Yes, I'm aware of that but we really do need the help. He hurt a woman, the mother of the infant the last time and I'm afraid he's going to do some real damage if we don't stop him."

Jim looked out the window, thinking, "OK, George, I know you wouldn't ask for help if you didn't really need it, so I'll give you three men for two weeks. Will that help?"

George rubbed his hands together, "Very good! Who will be in charge of it?"

"I'll put DCI Bridges on it. You know Billy don't you?"

George smiled, "I know him very well! He's a good man!"

"Good, well, let's get it set up and the guys'll be there in the morning to get started, OK?" George stood up. He was happy! He nodded as he went out.

When Liz saw him, she smiled because he was smiling, "We got it?"

George nodded and laughed, "We got it! Three guys, led by Billy Bridges.

Liz laughed, "Good old Billy!"

Last One

I'm not going to bore you with what went on, in the next two months. I took four more babies to order, two of them in Manchester, one in Portsmouth and one in North London. The police were everywhere in London, looking for the baby thief that was in the headlines of all the London newspapers! I was famous! Minh became a regular visitor, until one day she was gone. When I asked Gjin where she was, he said, "Don't worry, my boy, we have lots of nice pussy for you! Minh is gone to Paris where she will suck French cocks! Why don't you take one of our little girls? Look at little Lily; she is 12 years old and very experienced! I know that you will like her, my friend! I have her regularly and she actually, likes it, you know!"

I didn't answer him. He was constantly going

on about his little girls and every time I saw them, all I could see was my little sister! I sure didn't want anything to do with them, sexually. Sometimes, Lily and little Pina came over to my place to watch cartoons but I never wanted to touch them. Lily, especially, liked hot bubble baths, so I bought her some fragrant bath salts and she would soak for hours, while Pina sat with her and talked to her. Pina never wanted a bath. She said that when she took a bath at home, her brother would come in and she had to blow him, so she couldn't take a bath! Both of them were covered in bruises on their arms and on the inside of their thighs. Pina had welts on her back from being whipped. She told me that some of their 'clients' liked to whip her and Gjin got paid more for that.

One day, I was sitting on the sofa alone. Minh had shown me how to roast a chicken and make roast potatoes and a cheese omelet, so I was eating well and sometimes the girls would join me. I had just finished off some chicken when the mobile rang. Only one person called me on it, so I knew who it was and what she would want. I had almost £80 thousand saved up, now and after talking to Henry, I was thinking of taking the money and running away to America. He was sure that they might find me but I was getting tired of stealing the babies and I wanted to do something else. The excitement was gone! Her, as usual. "A black one, this time. A boy. Do it soon! Double the money, if you can do it by tomorrow!" She hung up. A black baby boy, by tomorrow!

    I'd spent some time walking around my old neighbourhood, usually at night. I met a guy, I knew by the name of Morty. He was 29 years old and had Down's Syndrome. His parents didn't want him and he had wandered down to King's Cross. The first time I saw him, he'd been sitting on the side of the canal, crying like a baby. I'd said, "Hey man, what's up with you?"

    He'd jumped to his feet and yelled, "Please don't hit me! I ain't done nothin' wrong!"

    I'd stood in front of him and looked at him. He was dressed in rags and he smelled terribly. "Don't worry my friend, I ain't gonna hurt you. Are you hungry?" He nodded, tears running down his cheeks, "Well, come with me, I'll get you a couple of burgers, OK?"

"You won't rape me?" He was trembling!

I laughed, "No, don't worry about that! Come with me. You can meet my girl, Kylie. She'll make sure you're alright."

We went to the burger bar and he inhaled two big burgers with all the trimmings! He was actually a very funny guy! I found Kylie and said, "Hey, Kylie, look what I found!"

She looked at Morty and said, "What the fuck is this, Satch?"

I laughed, "This is our new friend, Morty! He's a good guy!"

Kylie shook her head, "Typical! Always pickin' up strays! You need a shower, Morty! When's the last time you had one?"

Morty shrugged and smiled, "I don't know."

"Well, come on then." She looked at me and started to walk away. Morty followed her. She would make sure, that no one hurt him, anymore.

That had been, almost two years ago. Now, I saw Morty and he ran up to me, "Hi Satch. How are you, today?"

"I'm very good, Morty. I need you to do something for me, OK?"

"Sure Satch, anything you want."

"I'm going away and I need you take care of my box and my stuff, OK?" He'd always wanted my box.

"You want me to take care of your box? You mean I can use it?"

"That's it, exactly. You keep it and stay in it, until I get back."

"OK, Satch, thanks!" He was beaming!

Kylie saw me. She ran up to me, punched my shoulder and said, "You little prick! I told you I didn't want that fucking money!" She was joking of course! She had green hair now!

"Well, give it back then, you little fucker!"

She threw her arms around my neck and said, "So, are you back now? You wanna share my box? Blow job?"

I pushed her away, "No, I'm still in the flat. You should come and visit me. You could move in with me, if you want to."

"Mmm, mmm, no way! You're into somethin' too serious for me to take that chance; and don't tell me what you're doin'! I don't want to know! Have you noticed all the cops walkin' around here, now?" I nodded; I had seen them. "Well, they're lookin' for some young guy, that's been stealin' babies from their mothers! They showed us a photo of him. Whoever it is, better be careful!" She gave me a knowing look!

"Well, I know fuck all, about that, babe! Sounds the shit!"

"Oh, it's the shit alright, no doubt about that!"

"Well, OK, I gotta go. I'll see you around. I walked around the area for a while and once in a while, a cop would give me a close look as I went past him. They didn't speak to me but it was clear that they were looking for someone.

Now, where could I find a black, baby boy? I didn't have a car or even a driver's license. No credit card to rent one, even if I had a license. Up 'til now, I'd been using buses and other public transport to move around the city. I took the underground to Heathrow and I walked around the airport for a while. There were thousands of people with their luggage and of course, there were loads of families of all shapes and sizes. Cops with guns, everywhere. The underground had a station inside the airport, so if I took a baby from there, it would be easy to get away. I sat at a food kiosk and ate a burger and then I saw a young white woman with a little, black, baby in a buggy. She had her two suitcases with her and she was having a problem, pushing the buggy and keeping control of it, at the same time.

I got up and said to her, "Wow, looks like you need some help!"

She smiled at me, "Yes, I do, thanks. I need to get to Gate 33 to check-in." Foreign accent.

"Well, OK, I'll take the buggy and you handle the bags."

"Oh, thanks so much!"

We walked along; me pushing the buggy with the sleeping baby and her pulling the bags behind her. "This little one is sound asleep," I said, laughing.

"Yes, he's a good little boy. I'm his nanny. His parents are in Spain and I'm taking him to see them. We live in London."

A black, baby boy! I could see Gate 33 in the distance and I had been moving towards the underground exit. As we got alongside it, I could hear the beeping sound from the train, signaling that the door was closing, so I reached into the buggy, picked up the baby and sprinted down the stairs to the train! I got to it, just as the doors were closing! I could hear the nanny screaming and I was laughing, loudly! The train pulled away and I was on the move! The airport is full of CCTV cameras, so I knew that they would have a clear picture of me! I was excited! Would I get caught? I got off at the first station and ran to the taxi rank. I jumped into a taxi and told the driver to take me into London. I was thinking about the £20 thousand, I was going to get from this one and then it started to wake up. First, it started to whimper and then it started to cry. I could see the driver, looking at me in his mirror and I said, "I need to get this little guy home. His mother's waiting for him." The driver nodded but I could tell that he was suspicious.

The baby continued to cry and when the driver dropped me off, near my old train station, I ran from the car and went to Henry's. The baby was wailing and when he opened the door, he said, "Oh Christ, that's a noisy one, innit? Get in here laddie; come on, quick like!"

He looked at the baby and went to get some milk. Of course, he didn't have a baby bottle, so he put his fingers in the milk and dripped it into the baby's mouth as I had done with the one I stole in Southhall. It calmed the baby but I could see that it was still uncomfortable. "Probably shit itsel'!" Henry said. "I'll make the call, right now." He went away and I could hear him speaking. "They'll be here soon," he said.

It took them half an hour to reach us and when they got out of the car, she had a baby bottle. She picked up the crying baby, put the nipple into its mouth and looked at me and smiled. She went back to the car. He gave Henry his share; £6000 and he gave me £25,000! "Good job, Satch. This is a bonus!"

I stuck the cash in my shirt and when they were gone, Henry said, "Well, that's it for me matey! I'm done! My neighbour asked me, the other day about a cryin' baby, she'd heard down here, so I'm off! I gots enough money saved up to last me, out the rest of me days and I gots a wee place all ready for me, in the sun." He held out his hand for me to shake it, "I'll no see ye, again." I shook his hand and he handed me a small piece of paper, "This is their phone number. I know, ye'll need it. If they asks after me, ye dinna ken where I've gone, right?"

"You're right, I have no idea."

"OK, well, off ye go then."

I went out and he closed the door behind me. I never saw him again.

In Spain, next to his pool, at his villa, Wilf Sutton, the biggest drug dealer in the UK and the father of the black baby was sitting, with his wife, Sandra when his mobile rang, "Hello?" Screaming! "What the Hell? Who is this?" More screaming! He held the phone away from his ear and looked at Sandra. "Who is this?"

"Oh, Wilf, it's Mina! A guy stole Matthew,

right out of the buggy! He's gone!"

"What? What do you mean stole him? Where is he?"

"He's gone, Wilf! The guy stole him!"

Suddenly, Wilf calmed down, "Where are you, Mina?" Mina was crying. "Calm down now, love, come on, talk to me."

Mina sobbed and tried to calm down. "I was having trouble with my bags and the buggy and this young guy offered to help me. We were walking towards the gate and when we got to the underground, he grabbed Matthew, ran down the stairs and into the tube train! I tried to stop him but he was too fast! The cops were here and now, I don't know what to do!"

"Why were you alone?"

"Alf dropped me at the airport and I told him he could go home. He told me he had to see his girlfriend. She's gonna have a baby soon."

Wilf sat down, "You talked to the cops?"

"Yes, they were there in two seconds. They got on the train at the next stop but the guy was already gone. He took a taxi, into London, they think.

I'm so sorry, Wilf! There was nothing I could do!"

"OK, don't worry. I don't blame you!"

"Did they ask you, who's baby it is?"

She hesitated, "Yes, they did."

He waited, then said, "And what did you tell them?"

"I told them, it is your baby."

"You gave them my name?"

"Yes, I had to."

He shook his head. Fuck! "OK, honey, you did good."

"Oh Wilf, what will we do now? I am so worried!"

"You go home and wait for my call. Try not to talk to the cops, anymore, OK?"

"OK."

Trouble!

As I walked away from Henry's place, I started to think about what I was doing. London is covered by CCTV, in all parts of the city. There are thousands of them and there was no doubt that the police would have a clear picture of me from every angle and now that I'd taken a baby from Heathrow, which has even more cameras, they would be looking for me, everywhere. I had a lot of cash stored up, so I knew that I could go. The problem was; I didn't have a passport. I'd bought a laptop and had been going online playing games and such, so when I got to the flat, I went online to see the passport office and saw that I could apply online and pay for it with a debit card. I didn't have a bank account, so no debit card! Fuck!

I looked at one of the banks online and saw what I would need to set up a bank account and, of course, I didn't have any of that, either! No ID, no passport, no utility bills! I went out and knocked on

Gjin's door. "Ah, hello, my friend!"

"Hi Gjin; I need your help."

"My help? Well, come in, come in. Tell me what you need."

We went into the kitchen and the girls were at the table, eating their sandwiches, "Go out from here, girls! Satch needs something!" They smiled at me and took their food and went into my apartment. "Now, sit here, Satch. Tell me what you need."

"I need a passport. I want to go on holiday, to Portugal."

He laughed, "Is that all? That is easy! Come, stand up and let me take your photo. I will have a passport for you in three days! Portugal is a nice country! We have seven houses, full of young ones, there! You will like it and you can stay in one of the houses for free in Porto or Lisboa. You will be treated like a King!" I stood up and he took my photo with his phone. "OK, what is your name?"

"My name?"

"Of course, you pumpkin; I need your name for the passport!" He laughed!

"My name is Simon Atcheson."

He frowned, shook his head and handed the phone to me, "Put it in here." I typed my name into the phone and he said, "OK, good, I will have that for you in three days. £10,000, OK?"

"OK, sure, no problem. You bring me the passport, I'll give you the cash."

"OK, Simon, you will have it!"

I went back to my place and found the girls watching cartoons and laughing, as usual. I sat there, doing nothing for two days. The mobile rang! Fuck, not another one, already! "Hello?"

"Where did you get that baby?" It was her!

"Which baby?"

"The last one, the black one."

"At Heathrow; why, is there a problem?"

"We will come to you, later today."

"Is there a prob...?" She hung up. They're coming here? Doesn't sound good!

Two hours later, there was a knock on the door. When I opened it, Guzim was there with her and two very large guys, dressed in black suits. Oh, oh! The girls ran out of the room.

"Sit, Satch," Guzim said. I sat on the sofa and

he sat next to me. She, stayed standing, in her long, white fur coat and shiny black, high heels, looking around and wrinkling her nose, at the sparse furnishings. "We are here, because the baby you took from Heathrow is the son of Wilf Sutton." I'd never heard of him! "Do you know who that is?" I shook my head and shrugged. The name meant nothing to me. "He is the biggest drug dealer in the UK and he is very upset that you took his son!"

I shrugged, again; I didn't give a fuck! "So?"

"So?" He looked at her and the two guys and he laughed! "That's all you have to say?" Everyone, except her, laughed. I wasn't worried about the two big guys or Guzim; I was worried about her! She looked like she could kill me and not give it a second thought. I remembered what Henry had told me; she was the one in charge.

"Well, I don't have the baby, do I. You've got it! Why don't you just give it back?"

"We have offered that, but he wants the one that took the baby."

I wanted to scream and run out the door but the big guys were blocking it! "So, what're you gonna do, then?"

He looked at her, "Well, you are part of our team, so, of course you will be protected. Gjin has told me that your passport will be ready tomorrow, so we will put you on one of our private jets and you will go to Portugal as you have planned. We have a number of nice houses in Portugal, so you can stay in one of those until we can sort this out. If necessary, you can work from there. There are many babies in Portugal. When Gjin gives you your passport, you call us on the phone and we will come here to pick you up. Do not worry! We will take good care of you." He smiled at me, "Where is Henry?"

I was surprised and he saw it, "I have no idea. Isn't he, at his place?"

"No, we went to see him but his neighbours say, he is no longer there. Did he say anything to you?"

"No, he didn't say anything. He took his money from you and then I left him, as usual."

I could tell that he didn't believe me! "Well, should you hear from him, you let us know, yes?"

I looked at her and saw that she was

frowning at me. Fuck! One word from her and I'd be gone! I shrugged, "OK, sure, well, I guess that's it then."

He stood up, "Yes, that's it Satch. Until tomorrow."

When they were gone, I continued to sit there. Fuck them! When I had the passport, I'd be going, that's for sure but not with them! I had a lot of money stashed away and I would be taking that and going. Where to go, though? I'd never been outside of Britain and no doubt those fuckers would be watching for me to run; and now I had a big drug dealer looking for me! Of course, there were cops looking for me, everywhere too!

The next day, early, Gjin knocked on my door, "Here it is, my friend!" He handed me the new European passport. I opened it and saw my photo. "You like?"

"Yeah, looks good." I had the £10,000 ready for him. I handed it to him and he took it and smiled.

"Yes, very good, my friend! Now, you must call Guzim, yes?" I nodded. "Good, yes, our people will always take very good care of you; do not worry about anything!" He stood, looking at me. He was waiting for me to make the call.

I picked up the mobile and said, "Do you know the number?"

He smiled, took the phone from me, waited to hear it ringing and handed it back to me. "Yes?" Her!

"Satch!"

"Do you have it?"

"Yes." She hung up.

"Now, I wait here with you, my friend. I know you are in big trouble but do not think of running away, OK? We are a very large, global operation and we do not like it when our people go away. We have a very good team of people, who are employed, only to find the runaways. Be it the girls or children or anybody else in the organisation, you must not run because when you are found, and you will be found, you will be put into one of our houses, where the homos go and I know you will not like that! We make lots of porno films and even snuff films, where people are tortured in front of the camera. We have many clients, around the world, who like to see that and to do that, so you do not want to be in one of those films, now, do you! This is where Minh went, actually. She tried to go home to see her mother and after Paris, she went into a film.

Minh! Sweet girl! A knock on the door. Gjin opened it, "Ah, here you are, Lorik! Satch is here and ready with his shiny, new passport!"

Lorik, one of the big guys that had been with them, yesterday, came into the room, "Let's go." He said.

I got up and Gjin shook my hand, "It has been good to know you, young Simon! Be well! I do not think we will see you, again but we will think of you!"

I'd packed the few clothes I had and all of my cash; £100,000 into a small backpack. I picked it up and went out the door and saw, little Lily standing in their doorway, "Goodbye Satch! See you!" Sasha, pulled her inside the flat and slapped her! Fucking bitch! Poor little kid!

"OK, Lily, see you."

A long drive to a small airport and I'm alone, in a private jet; I'd never flown before; going to – I don't know where; Portugal?

Hunting

"Jules, get Harris and get over here, fast!"

"Sure boss, what's up?"

"Get over here, now!"

Wilf Sutton closed the phone and went to sit on his patio. He was, still in Spain at his villa. He was drinking a beer and felt like he could murder someone! He was the biggest drug dealer in the UK and the thought of someone stealing his son, had him screaming! He had so many enemies and rivals around the UK and in a lot of places around the world, that he couldn't, begin to think of who would have taken him. He'd had to struggle all his life because he was a black man and growing up in Brixton, he'd been very poor. In spite of it all, he'd succeeded! He was the boss!

He would have to deal with Alf, his old and

trusted friend, Alf; known him since primary school. He had dropped Mina off at the airport to go and see his bitch, instead of going into the airport with her! Old friend or no, he'd be gone before the sun went down! Stupid fucker!

His wife, Sandra came out to sit next to him. "I got some really bad news, babe," he said. She'd been with him, in all their years, coming up through the business and she'd never let him down. They had three children, two of them girls, Betsy and Louisa and little David was the latest one; 10 months old. He was the heir to everything. The only boy!

She looked alarmed and said, "What? What is it?"

He leaned forward and took her hand, "Someone, snatched David from Heathrow!"

She jumped to her feet! "Snatched him? What the fuck do you mean?"

Wilf stood up, "Mina was walking through the airport and some young guy ran up and grabbed David out of the buggy. He ran into the tube and disappeared!"

She put her hands on her head and

screamed! "But where is he? Where was Alf?" She burst into tears! Wilf put his arms around her and she pushed him away! "You have to find him! Oh my God!"

The doorbell rang and Wilf went to answer it, "Come in, guys. I need to talk to you." Sandra ran up the stairs, crying loudly!

Jules watched her run by and he looked at Wilf, "What's up, boss?"

They went out to the patio, "Sit," Wilf said. When they were all seated, he said, "Somebody snatched David from Heathrow."

Jules looked at Harris, "Snatched him? Where was Alf?"

"Yeah, snatched him! Some young fucker ran up to Mina and grabbed the little guy out of his buggy and then he jumped onto the tube and left! Alf dropped off Mina and went to see his girl."

Harris shook his head, "Stupid fucker!"

"Yeah, that's what I said. I need you to put a round in his head, later. Right now, we have to find out who took him and where he is, now, so we can get him back. It could have been, any one of a hundred people, you both know that. There's a lot of people out there that want my action, so let's get everybody movin' and find out where he is. We got people all over the country, so we should be able to find out somethin'. It's one thing, if it's business but it could be anything."

"We got them Albanian people traffickers there, causin' all kinds of trouble." Harris said. "They're stealin' kids and sellin' them and they put them in porn films too. Lotsa heat because of them!"

Wilf stretched, "Well, whatever, put the word out and let's see what's what. We'll fly back to London today."

The police task force was set up in a hurry. DC Mason and his partner Liz were now part of a five person task force, dedicated to finding the baby thief that was plaguing the country. They had his photo and a rough location for him in London but no solid leads. They had constables out, all over the country, hunting high and low but so far, they had nothing. It had been almost three months and babies were reported, being stolen in a number of different locations; Portsmouth, Manchester and, of course London. There were, usually baby and child thefts but in this case, they were looking for one specific suspect; the young guy in the T shirts!

DC Len Hamblin came in, "Got another one."

George sat back in his chair and said, "Shit, where now?"

"Heathrow."

"Heathrow? That place is crawling with security! How the Hell did he snatch a baby from there?"

Hamblin looked at the paper, he had in his hand, "Our guy ran up to a nanny, took the kid and jumped onto the tube. Before the nanny could do anything, he was gone. Got off at the next stop and took a taxi into the London. They've spoken to the driver and he says he dropped the guy off, outside King's Cross Station."

"Did the nanny know anything?"

Hamblin smiled, "It's the son of Wilf Sutton."

George grabbed the paper and read it! "Well,

fuck me! This is gonna cause a stir!" He smiled. "We're going to have a lot of help, now! Our boy fucked up, this time! Sutton's got almost as many people on the street as we do and they don't have to follow any rules!"

He went out to the task force room, "Attention everyone!" Everyone stopped what they were doing and looked at him. He waved the paper and said, "We just got a big boost! Wilf Sutton's baby boy got snatched by our guy from Heathrow! Him and his people'll be hunting, everywhere for him!" He looked into Billy's office and saw that it was empty.

Liz, used work the drug squad, so she knew a lot of people in the business. She looked at George, "Come on, George; I've got an idea." She took some of the photos and he followed her.

"Where are we going?"

"To a pub, I know, that Wilf's people work out of." When they got inside the pub, she found Sally, a drug addict she knew. "Come here, Sally."

"I got nothin' Liz, I promise, I don't!"

Liz smiled. She could see that Sally was high. "That's OK, babe. I got something for you."

Sally hung back and looked at the exit. George moved to block her path and she slumped back into her chair, "OK, so, what do you got for me?"

Liz took out the photos, "Tell Wilf, that this is the guy that took David."

Sally took the photos, puzzled, "Who's David and who's Wilf?"

"Never mind that. Just make sure, he has these today."

"But I don't know, no one called Wilf."

"I know you don't, but just make sure he has these today. He'll pay you, well for them, I promise you."

"But, I don't know, no one called Wilf."

"I know honey, I know you don't."

Running!

Yes, the plane flew to Portugal, Porto, in fact and when I got out of the jet, the heat hit me! There was a guy, Lorik's twin, waiting for me. "Mr. Satch, I am Fatos. You will come with me to the house, now." He opened the door of a big, black car and I got in with my backpack. The car went through the Portuguese countryside and we finally came to a small town called, Penafiel. The name meant nothing to me and we arrived at a big house with a high wall around it.

I got out of the car and Fatos said, "Follow me, Mr. Satch. We go inside, out of this heat!" Same accent as Gjin.

We went into the house, into a large parlour with paintings on the walls. It was airy and well furnished, with a large baby grand piano in it. There were a lot of big plants, like palm trees and the patios doors opened out to a big garden with a swimming pool. It was a real mansion! Next to the pool, were some very good looking women and young girls; about twenty, in total, ranging in age from 12 years old, to some, in their teens and twenties. Most of them were topless and some of them were nude! I noticed, three young guys, too. They were, also nude!

When they saw me, they smiled at me and a couple of them, said hello. They, obviously thought I was there to fuck them. Fatos came out, "Ladies, this is Mr. Satch. He works here. Please be nice to him, while he is here!"

One of the girls, about 20 or so; a tall, thin, girl with strawberry blonde hair, blue eyes, small breasts and no pubic hair, stood up, "Sit here, next to me, Satch. I am Elena. Please, come, take off your clothes and sit close to me." She came over to me and started to unbutton my shirt!

"I want to put my bag in my room and take a shower, OK?" I said, taking her hands away. I went back into the house, picked up my pack and said to Fatos, "Where is my room, Fatos? I want to take a shower."

"Ah, OK, Mr. Satch, you follow me, now."

We went upstairs and he opened the door to a large room, overlooking the pool. "You will stay in this room. I do not know how long you will be here but you may sleep here, OK?"

"OK, sure, thanks, Fatos." I saw the gun in his coat as he went past me. He was a very tough looking guy! Albanian for sure.

I looked out the window and I could see, everyone around the pool. What a fucking sight! Well tanned, naked and scantily clad girls and women, everywhere! I took off my clothes and took a shower. I laid on the bed and the next thing I knew, I woke up, with someone was giving me a blow job! I opened my eyes and pushed the person away from me! I looked up and saw Elena, kneeling next to me on the bed with a surprised look on her face! "You do not like that, Satch?"

I was as surprised, as she was, "Oh, I like it, alright! I was surprised, that's all! I didn't expect it!"

I sat up and looked at her. She was a nice looking girl.

She reached for my erect cock and said, "Do you want some more, now?"

I had been near and around prostitutes, my whole life because of my mother. All of her friends were working girls and we had had them in our house, throughout my whole childhood and of course, when I lived on the street, they were everywhere. Kylie works the streets to support her habit and they were many, many others. I understand their mentality and I know that just about all of them would do anything else, if they could find out what that is. I was sure that this, Elena was working as a sex slave and I had no intention of doing anything to make her life any worse than it probably, already was. I held my arm up to her and said, "Come here and lie down next to me." She reached for my cock which was no longer erect and I said, "No, not that; just lie here, next to me."

She, warily, laid down beside me and I put my arm around her and held her to me. "So, what do you want from me, if not that?"

Quietly, I said, "I don't want anything from you. Just lay here and take a break, OK?" I felt her relax and I drifted back to sleep and thought about Minh. Sweet girl!

When I woke up, it was dark and Elena was still lying next to me, breathing softly. She was asleep. What woke me, was someone knocking on my door, "Mr. Satch, we will eat dinner soon, OK? Elena, you must go to the room, now!"

Elena woke up, "Yes, yes, Fatos, I will be there!" She sat up and looked at me, "I must go to the room, now, Satch." She kissed my cheek. "I will tell the others, what you did today. You will have many visitors, now!" She got off of the bed, stretched and went out of the room, still completely naked.

I got dressed and went downstairs. The house, was truly a mansion! On the floor, I was on, there were doors on all sides of the corridor. It was like a hotel and had another floor above. Big house! I saw Fatos, "Ah good, come with me and meet the senor, Mr. Satch. He knows of you!"

He led me into a big, dining room with a large, wooden table surrounded by chairs. There were a lot of plants in the room and it was well lit. At the head of the table was a man in his fifties with white hair and a goatee and moustache. He was dressed in a colourful, satin dressing gown. Fatos said to him, "Senor Anibal Costa, this is Mr. Satch from London."

The man stood up and motioned me, to a chair next to him, "Come in Satch, sit here next to me." He held out his hand and I shook it. "It is good that you are here," he said. "The house is yours while you are here and I hope that you like what is here." Accent; Portuguese?

I smiled. I'd never seen anything like it! I'm a street kid, remember! "Yes, sir, it is a very nice house," I looked at the girls and women and said, "and very well furnished."

He smiled, while someone put a plate, in front of me, "Please, I'm sure you are hungry. Please, eat some of this wonderful Portuguese food and fill your glass with this very good wine! There is warm bread there, also. The food smelled fantastic!"

I did as he said and found that I was very hungry! I ate roast veal with roasted potatoes and vegetables and I drank a good bit of the wine, as well! The bread was great! An excellent meal! "Now, Guzim has explained your problem to me and we will do our best to be sure that you do not have any problems here. As far as we know, no one knows you are here, yet. Of course, the man that is looking for you, also has excellent resources but we are hoping that you will be good here."

I had just finished my third glass of wine and was feeling very relaxed but what he said, made me sit up a bit straighter! "Do you think he'll find me here?"

"No, I do not think he will, but we will take all necessary precautions, anyway. You are a valuable part of the organisation and have made us a lot of money, so we will protect you as well as we can. You are family!" The last fucking thing, I wanted to be! "Now, we will soon have a houseful of clients to use the girls, so you may do as you wish." He called out something in his language; Portuguese I guessed and one of the young girls brought us sniftersful of brandy. "This is Portuguese, five star brandy; Macieira! I know you will like it!" I took a sip and he was right; the brandy was excellent!

Wilf and his crew were at his house in North London.

Jules. "Got Sally here, boss."

"Sally? Tell her to fuck off! I'm busy now!"

Jules came back with some photos in his hand, "She gave me these and says she's got a message for you, about David."

Wilf looked at the photos, "David? Send her in." Sally came into the room, trembling with fear! She smelled badly! "What you got Sally?"

"That cop woman gave me these photos and told me to bring them to you. She said that this is the guy what took David."

He looked more closely at the photos and frowned. He laid the photos on the table, leaned forward and he was really looking at her, now! "Tell me what woman and tell me everything she said."

"That's it! It was that cop woman; that Liz woman, the one that used to arrest me all the time. She said; take these to Wilf and tell him that this is the guy that took David." She was almost peeing herself, she was so afraid! She still didn't know who David was! "She said, you'd pay me for them but you don't have to, if you don't want to. I don't need payin' Wilf; I don't, you know!" She was grinding her teeth and she wanted to run out of the room!

Wilf smiled, "Don't worry; you done good, honey. Jules, give Sally a nice big bag for her trouble." He handed one of the photos to Sally, "And, now I want you to show this to everybody and tell them, that whoever can tell me who this fucker is, I'll set them up good and proper, you got me?"

Sally, trembling but feeling happier, knowing she was going to get some free drugs, took the photo and said, "Aye, I'll do that! Never fear, Wilf, I'll help you, alright!" She still had no idea who David was!

Constable Lindsey Merrick was doing her usual job, canvassing with the photos of the baby thief. She'd asked hundreds of people if they'd seen him and so far, nothing. She was bored, hot and feeling very irritable. No one knew him, had seen him or had any idea who he was. She'd gone, all over the last known area on the CCTV, maybe fifty times and now she was back at the Regent's Canal next to King's Cross Station – again! Same walkers, cyclists, artists and street people, as usual. Boring! Ask this man, ask this woman, ask these druggies, hippies, musicians, homeless people – again! She walked up to a big guy with Down's Syndrome. She'd seen him many times and had ignored him, thinking he wouldn't know anything. "Have you seen this man?"

The guy, Morty, looked at the photo and said, "Hey, that's Satch! I know him! I'm takin' care of his box for him!" He looked very proud and smiled widely!

Lindsey couldn't move! What? "You know him?"

Morty took the photo and kissed it! "This is my best friend! He gave me his box! Can I keep this picture, please? He's my best friend!"

She switched on her radio mike. "Constable Lindsey Merrick, here. I've got a lead on our baby thief."

"Right, Constable Merrick. Where are you?"

"Regent's Canal next to The Lighterman at King's Cross. I've got a good lead, here with me."

"Stand by, we'll have someone from the task force there in a jiffy. Keep your lead there."

"Roger, will do."

When Morty heard what she said into the mike, he started to walk away. He still had the photo of Satch in his hand and he wanted to get out of there! Lindsey put her hand on his arm, "No, no, you have to stay here, OK, mate? Just, for a few minutes."

Morty was having none of it! "Nope, I gotta go now! Kylie's waitin' for me, now; I gotta go!" He started to cry and to move away. Lindsey tried to stop him but he was twice her weight and he, easily pulled away from her. He started to run, yelling, "She's trying to rape me! Help!" All of the people in the area looked at them. Some of them were laughing and others, the homeless people that knew Morty, started to move in their direction. Morty was important to them and although Lindsey was police, they were going to make sure he got away. Slowly, one by one, they moved to block her way and as she pushed through them, she saw Morty being led away by a young, blonde girl. When she got to where they'd been, they were gone! She ran around looking for him but he was gone!

Underground

Wilf sat on his patio in London, sipping coffee and looking at the photos that Sally had given him. He didn't know the guy. He called Jules, "Yes, boss?"

He held up one of the photos, "I'm gonna make 100 copies of this photo and I want you and everyone else to distribute them around the country. I want this fucker caught, now! No fuckin' about! Whoever, can tell me who he is and where he is, gets 50 grand, no questions asked!"

"50 grand, boss?"

"That's what I said!" He went into his office, put the best photo into the photocopier and pushed the button. The copies started to come out of it. He stood next to the machine with his arms crossed and waited. Jules was watching him, nervously. He was thinking, how, he wouldn't want to be the guy in the photo! When the machine stopped, Wilf took the copies and handed them to Jules, "Now, two things. First, get these out to everyone on the street and tell them to get copies made. I want them all over the country by the mornin'! No fuckin' about! Second, you and Harris go to Alf's place and put a bullet in his brain! I don't give a fuck what you do with the body, just make sure he ain't alive! Now go!"

"Yes boss!"

The Next Move

Two weeks went by. I spent all day, laying beside the pool, in the sun and, after dinner when the clients arrived, I went up to my room or for a walk around the small town. There wasn't much, except a few cafes and bars, so I kept, pretty much to my room. When Elena told everyone that I wasn't interested in having sex with them; slowly but surely, my room became a gathering point. The girls, especially the youngest ones, the 10 – 12 year olds started to watch cartoons in my room during the day, just like the little girls in London and because I had an over sized, king size bed, there were mornings when I would wake up with 3 and sometimes 4 girls, sleeping in my bed!

Elena, was constantly by my side and I was starting to like her. She started to talk to me, one morning. She'd come into my room, after 4 AM when the clients left and when we woke up in the morning, she was in my arms. I kissed her cheek and felt her lovely, naked body against me. She felt, really good! She woke up and looked at me, "Well, good morning, man! Did you sleep well?"

"Yes, I really did. I like wakin' up with you in my arms!"

She wriggled closer to me and smiled, "Mmm, me too. It feels natural, doesn't it!" I nodded. She sat up, "You know, I have been with these people since I was 11 years old. I have been moved to 12 different countries and been in porno films, when I was younger and now, here I am, 21 years old and still getting fucked for money by 10 – 15 men every night!"

"Where do you come from?"

"I am from Montenegro, Budva. My father and my brother started to have sex with me when I was 9 years old and then my father owed some money because of gambling, so he sold me to these Albanians. They have had me, ever since. I can hardly read and I never know when I will be moved again."

"Haven't you ever tried to get away?"

"Oh yes, of course, when I was younger but somehow they always found me and brought me back. They have people, that only look for runaways. They are very good at their work! It is impossible! You need a lot of money and a passport and everything! It is impossible for me! I know that one day, they will take me to one of their snuff houses, probably in Romania, where they do that, like they have done to other girls and they will take money from someone to torture me to death in front of the cameras. Some clients like to do that! I have seen the films! Always, girls my age! We are too old, you see!"

She was talking, like these things were normal! "Do you want to get away?"

She looked at me, wide eyed, "Of course I do, but I do not, have even a small amount of money! Do you know what it costs to buy a passport? You need to be rich!"

I pulled her down to me and kissed her. "I have money."

She sat up and stared at me! "You are working for them, aren't you! You will tell them, I want to get away from this shit!" She tried to get out of the bed but I held onto her and slowly pulled her back down to me. I put my arms around her and said, "Yes, I do work for them but the things I do have nothing to do with what you do. I am here, in hiding from a very bad man and I would never tell them anything, you tell me, OK?"

She started to cry, quietly, "Oh thank you, Satch. I love you, you know." She kissed my neck and held me tightly.

Suddenly, the door burst open and Asha, 10 years old, Suzie, 12 years old and Daisy, 11 years old, all dressed in pajamas, came dashing into the room! They jumped onto the bed and started yelling and screaming and tickling me and Elena! We jumped up and grabbed them and started to wrestle with them! That went on for quite a while and then, Asha took the remote and put on the cartoon channel, like she did, every morning in my room. I pulled Elena down to me, put my arms around her and whispered, "I love you, too, babe." She made a purring sound and we laid there, watching the cartoons. We got up, after an hour, listening to the girls laughing at the TV and we took a shower together like we did, almost every morning. We went to breakfast and then out to the pool. About lunch time, I said to Elena, "Come up to my room." I had bought a mobile phone in the town and when we got to the room, I said to her. "Stand over there, so I can take your photo."

She was puzzled, "But why do you want a photo of me."

"Because I'm going into the town to find out if I can buy a passport for you."

She looked really frightened, "But you cannot do that, Satch! My God, if they ever found out, both of us would be sent to one of the bad houses, in Romania, where they make the films!" She covered her face and went towards the door.

I pulled her back and said, "No, come, stand over there by the wall, so that I can take your photo. I'll go into the town and if I find someone, it will be OK and if not, it won't matter, will it."

Very reluctantly, she went and stood beside

the wall. The sun was shining into the room and I snapped three photos of her. I showed them to her and she chose the second one, "Use this one; it looks the best."

I went into the town, to a small square, where I'd noticed that some homeless people were. I knew all about these people! They were my neighbours, like all homeless people are, all over the world. Over the nine years, I'd been living on the streets, I'd met hundreds of them, in London, from everywhere on the planet! They always knew where to buy dope, booze or anything else a person could need, including passports and travel papers. I went up to them and sat, against a wall, next to them. One guy, German looking, slid down next to me and said, "So, what do you need?" German accent.

I didn't look at him, "Passport."

"You got cash?"

"Pounds."

"You'll need a lot." Still, not looking at me.

"A thousand for you and whatever the passport costs."

"You got a photo?"

"You got a phone?"

He nodded, "What's your number?" I gave it to him and he phoned me. "OK, in five minutes, you text me the photo. I'll come back here in two hours and you bring the cash for the deposit."

"How much?"

He laughed, "This is Portugal, man! Could be anything! Bring enough!" He got up and left the square.

Could I trust this guy? I guess I'd find out in two hours. I sent him Elena's photo in a text message. I went to my room, counted out £11,000 and put it inside my pillow case. I went down for lunch and a little swim and then I laid next to Elena on the patio. The three little girls came over and sat on top of me, so I stood up and threw them all, screaming, into the pool, then I dived in after them! They were hysterical! We played for a while and then I went and showered, dressed, took the cash and went back to the square. I sat on a bench and very soon, the German came over to me and sat next to me. "OK, he wants £6000 for the passport, ready tomorrow. He wants half now." He didn't look at me.

"Do you want to be killed?"

He laughed, "Killed? No!"

"Well, killed you will be, if you try to fuck me, OK?"

"Don't worry, my friend, I would never do that! You are safe!"

I went into the toilets and counted out the money; 500 for him, 3000 for the guy. I sat next to him, looked around, to be sure no one was looking and I passed the cash to him, "Half of yours and half of his."

He said, "7, tomorrow night, here." He stood up and walked out of the square.

'Well, there goes £3500'! I thought, as I walked back to the house.

I spent the rest of the day, laying next to the pool and then, had dinner, as usual. I went to bed and thought about Elena's passport. Where would we go? It sounded like she knew Europe really well, so I guessed that she would have some good suggestions. I went to sleep and woke up in the morning with 5 young girls in my bed! I threw a blanket over them and wouldn't let them out of the bed! They were screaming and going crazy trying to get away and when Asha broke loose, she jumped on top of me and forced me to let the others go, too!" They ran out of the room and I laid there, thinking that it was like a nursery school!

Nothing much happened during the day, so I went out to the square, just before 7:00. I had the rest of the money with me and I hoped that I hadn't been ripped off! I kept watching the digital clock on the Pharmacy wall and it slowly went past 7:00 to 7:30 and still no German! Looks like the fucker robbed me! At 7:45, he came into the square. He saw me and came over to sit beside me, "£3500 my friend!" No, sorry I'm late or fuck all! He took an envelope out of his shirt and held his hand out. I took the envelope and handed him the money. He got up and went out of the square. I walked back to the house, stopping for a beer, in one of the cafes. When I got to the house, there were the usual collection of men there, to fuck the girls. I caught Elena's eye and smiled at her, nodding upstairs. I went up to my room, locked the door and opened the envelope. A European passport in the name of

Joana Marconi from Naples; Elena's photo! It looked perfect!

I hid it under the mattress, unlocked the door and laid on the bed, and waited for Elena. I fell asleep and some time in the night, I felt her getting into bed. She was naked, as usual. "Did you lock the door?"

"Yes, I did."

I reached under the mattress and took out the passport, "This is for you, Joana." I handed it to her.

"But, I am Elena!" The room was lit by a very high, very bright moon. She opened the passport and put her hand up to her mouth, "Satch! Oh my God, Satch!" She was whispering, loudly! She shook the passport in my face! "Look at this! It is me!" She fell onto the bed and buried her face in the pillow and started to cry, really hard! I put my hand on her neck and kissed her cheek. She lifted her face up and said, very quietly, "Oh my, man, look what you did for me! I will love you forever, now! Oh my, oh my!" She held the passport up, so that it could catch the moonlight, "Senorina Joana Marconi." Then, she started to speak, fluent Italian and then, said in English, "I was in a house in Napoli for almost a year, you know! I speak a lot of different Italian dialects. Many Italian men fucked me and wanted me to speak with them in their own language, so when I was sucking them or fucking them, they could have a better time, you know!" She said something else in Italian and then threw her arms around my neck! "Now, I will be Joana!"

"Where do you want to go?"

"Go?"

I laughed, "Yes, go! You have a passport, so you can go anywhere in the world. Where do you want to go?"

She sat up with a look of panic on her face! "I do not know! Go?" I nodded and mouthed, 'go'. "Go?" she said, again. I nodded, again. "I do not know but we must go somewhere, mustn't we!" I nodded, again. This was turning into a comedy show! Suddenly, she threw the passport on the bed, "No! Oh my God, Satch! We cannot go anywhere, that they cannot find us! Everyone who leaves, eventually gets found!"

"Did those people have money?" She shook her head. "Passports?" She shook her head. She was looking like little Asha, now. "Did they have me to help them?" She shook her head. "So, you have a passport and money and me to help you. You can go anywhere in the world."

She threw herself back onto the bed and snuggled next to me, "Do you want to fuck me, now? I, only had two clients tonight, so I am ready for you, if you want me." We made love for over an hour and it was very good! We both came and it was excellent! I took the passport, put it back under the mattress and we went to sleep.

Connection

DC George Mason, DC Liz Dawson and DC Harold Lawson arrived on the scene within half an hour of getting the call. They found Constable Merrick, easily and George said to her, "Hello Constable Merrick, what do you have for us?"

Lindsey sighed, "Well, I had a man here, that said that he knows this guy in the photo. He called him Satch."

"You had him here?"

"Yes, I did. He was here and then, when I started to question him, he ran away. I tried to catch him but a few people around here, accidentally, on purpose got in my way!" She scowled at some of the homeless people. The were not bothered by her, at all. They were used to police 'prowling around' as they called it!

"So, where did he go?" Liz asked.

"I followed him as far as the pub and then he was gone. He told me that Satch had asked him to take care of his box, whatever that means!" She was upset that she'd lost the guy.

"So, what does this guy look like?" Harold asked her. He had his notebook out.

"Big guy, white, fat and he has Down's Syndrome. Smelly. Obviously, homeless."

George looked around, "Lots of CCTV here. Let's go and see if we can see him, on any of these cameras."

Kylie was sitting with Morty, beside their boxes. Morty had Satch's photo and he was looking at it, lovingly, "This is our good friend, Satch!" he said and then he laughed. "That lady gave it to me! This is my pitcher! I'm keepin' it! Satch gave me his box to take care of!"

Kylie smiled, "Yep, it's your picture alright. You're gonna have to hide now, OK, Morty?"

"Hide? Hide where?" He looked confused.

"Well, do you want the lady to come here and take the picture away from you?"

He held the photo close to his chest and frowned, "This is my pitcher of my best friend, Satch! He's lettin' me stay in his box until he comes back! Nobody's gonna take this pitcher away from us!" He held up the photo, "This is Satch, my best friend!"

Kylie stood up. She was aware of the CCTV cameras and she usually ignored them. She knew that the police would be back to find Morty and that they would use the CCTV to find him. She knew of a place near the canal where there were no cameras. "Come on, Morty, stand up. We're goin' for a boat ride, OK?"

Morty jumped up and said, "Yeah! I like boats! Sometimes Willis lets me sit on his boat on the canal!"

"Well, we're goin' to see Willis right now, OK? We're goin' on his boat for a ride." She knew that Willis would want, at least a blow job to help them but she had to get Morty away from the cops. They walked to the canal and found him. "Hey Willis, how's it goin'?"

"Oh, it's goin' OK, honey. What do you need?" He was stoned, as usual.

"I need to go up the canal for a bit. Morty's got some trouble." Short form, for police trouble!

"Well, that's no problem. You gonna pay me?"

She put her finger in her mouth and sucked it. He smiled and winked at her. "Sure, no problem," she said.

Willis laughed, "Well, what the fuck! All aboard!"

"Get on the boat and go inside, Morty."

Morty was excited! "I never been inside one of these boats before!" He climbed aboard and went inside.

"Now, you just sit there quiet, OK Morty?" Kylie said.

Morty held the photo close to his chest and said, "Look at this, Satch! We're inside a boat!"

Willis untied the mooring lines, started the engine and got onto the boat, ready to steer it up the canal. Kylie was looking inside and he reached out and felt her bum. She turned to him and smiled. They went up the canal.

George and the others went to the CCTV Centre and looked at the footage. "That's him," Lindsey said. They were looking at a large man with a blue shirt and very dirty jeans. He was wearing sandals and they could see that his feet were black!

"Definitely, got Down's Syndrome!" Liz said.

They watched him run away and they saw how the homeless people got in Lindsey's way. "He's one of them, that's for sure! Those folks, only help their own!" George said. They watched him on a different camera, go up the short hill and they saw a young woman, help him to get out of sight. Two cameras later and there they were, sitting beside two large cardboard boxes. "That must be their places!" Harold said.

"Yep, I know, exactly where that is!" Lindsey said. "I've been patrolling this area for over a year. I know where it is."

"It's surprising that you don't know our guy." Liz said.

She looked at Liz, "Well, you know Liz, there's just so many of them. If they don't do anything to attract attention to themselves, they're invisible!"

"Well, OK, then, let's get over there!" George said.

They left the CCTV Centre and walked to the place where the boxes were. There was no one around, so they had a Constable, tape the area off and they went to get a search warrant. Even a cardboard box needed a search warrant, if someone was living in it!

When Willis stopped the boat, he asked Morty to sit outside. He told him to watch and make sure no one came to steal the boat. He went inside with Kylie and she gave him a blow job.

"We sent them photos, out, boss," Jules told Wilf.

"And what about Alf?"

"Done! He knew it was comin'! No fight! He knew that he fucked up! His girlfriend freaked out, 'cause of their baby but there was nothin' she could do about it! He's in the woods now."

"Good, well, shit happens! Anything on the photos, yet?"

"Nope, not yet."

When Lindsey had been chasing Morty at the canal, two young black guys, street kids and small time dope dealers, Freddy and Jamie, had been sitting nearby, waiting for some customers. They saw Morty run past, holding the photo and it caught their attention. They knew it was Satch. A guy they knew had given them the same photo, earlier and said that Wilf was looking for him. They hadn't paid any attention to it, but, as they saw Morty run past, they got interested. Freddy looked at the photo, "That fuckin' goof, Morty's, got the same picture, man and that cop's chasin' him! They want Satch!"

Freddy laughed! "Yeah, that's him, alright! He don't touch dope, he don't drink and Kylie told me, he don't fuck, either!"

"Well, let's get over to his box and see if he's there!" They ran over to the boxes and were surprised to see the police tape around them. They walked past and Freddy said, "Better call, Wilf." They never called Wilf! He was too scary for them! They got their drugs from one of Wilf's dealers and they made just enough money to survive. Jules had once told them, to never call Wilf, unless it was an emergency!

"Well, you know what Jules told us! Better, we call him, instead. Don't wanna get Wilf pissed off with us!" Freddy nodded. Jamie dialed, Jules' number, "Hey Jules, it's Jamie."

"Yeah, what's up?" It was Wilf.

"We know the guy in the photo, man!"

"You know him?"

"Who is this?" Suddenly, he knew he was talking to Wilf! "Oh, ah, this is Jamie!" He almost fell over with shock!

"Jamie? You know the guy in the photo?"

"Yeah, me and Freddy know him."

A long pause, while Jamie sweated; finally, "Who is he?"

"His name's Satch. He's a homeless guy. Lives in a box near King's Cross."

"Homeless guy, huh. You know, where he is now?"

"No, don't know; he ain't been around for a while."

"Where are you now?"

"We went past his box but the cops are there, so now we're back at the canal near King's Cross."

"The cops know about him?"

"Yeah, I guess they do. They're lookin' for him."

"Stay right there. Don't move! I'll be there soon and if you're right, you got a big pay day comin'! Stay there!"

"Yes sir!" He closed the phone.

Freddy grabbed him! "Was that Wilf?" Jamie nodded. "So, what'd he say?"

"He told me, to stay right here! He's comin' here with a big pay day for us!"

"Fuck man, I hope that don't mean a big pay day!" He pointed at his temple and pulled the trigger!

An Escape Plan

The next morning, there was a loud banging on the door of my room! I got up, naked and opened the door. Four, almost nude young girls, wearing little bikinis, ran into the room and Asha took the remote and turned the TV to the cartoon channel! I yelled, "Hey, why don't you girls ever watch the big TV downstairs?"

Asha looked at me and stuck her tongue out, "We don't have to, that's why!" She turned back to the TV, with the others, laughing. I could see their bruises.

I ran over to her, picked her up, which caused her to scream and I ran with her to the balcony of the room, climbed over the railing and jumped into the pool! She was screaming the whole time! As soon as we hit the water, the other girls jumped off of the balcony and landed next to us! Panic in the pool, after that!

Elena was gone, when I got back to the room and when I checked for the passport, I found that she had left it. I was sure, that she was too frightened to take it!

When I got to the breakfast table, Anibal was there. "So, Satch, you are doing well, here, I see!" He was smiling, widely.

I laughed, "Yes, it is very good to be here. I get along with everyone and I'm getting a very good tan!"

"Are you bored yet?"

"Bored? No, not at all. I'm enjoying myself too much!"

"And what about our girl, Elena?"

"Oh, she's a very nice person."

"Yes, yes she is. I can see that she likes you."

"Yes, I think she does."

"Well, do not get too close to her. She will be moved to Romania, to make a film, soon."

Romania! Oh no! Snuff films! "Does she know that?"

"No, not yet. We will tell her next week. She is past her prime now, you see. She has been with us for a very long time and our clients like the young ones, much more. She only did two clients last night. That is a very poor show. We have the little ones and the clients prefer them. We have a nice place in Romania for the older girls."

I nodded and ate my food. There was a lump in my throat and I was having some difficulty breathing. My impulse control had been very good, this whole time but, as I said, when I felt stress, it started to come back! It was coming back now! I needed to scream! I excused myself and went to the room. I laid on the bed and screamed into the pillow, over and over again! I wanted to smash something! I laid there, trying to catch my breath. I'd have to go and see the German, again! We needed to get out, now!

Anibal, was sitting beside the pool, reading a book and he looked up, as I passed him. I smiled and pulled my hat down tighter. I walked, calmly into the town. When I got to the square, the German wasn't there. I sat in a café and had a beer. I drank it, slowly and as I ordered a second one, the German appeared. He nodded to me and I pointed, with my head at the bench we had sat on, together. He went to the bench and I joined him. "I need to leave here with Joana, tonight."

"So, why don't you go?"

"Can't; need help to get away. Got no car."

"What time?"

"After 3 AM."

"You want to go far?" I nodded. "OK, come here with £1000 and I'll arrange it. You will be safe."

Discovery

Wilf and Jules went to the canal to meet with Freddy and Jamie. They found them, sitting with their backs against a wall, looking around, nervously. Wilf sat next to Freddy, "So, tell me," he said.

Freddy had never met Wilf and now that he had, he could see what they meant when they talked about him. Wilf was black, six foot six and heavily built with very large muscles. He looked very tough, because he was. He ran a large drug empire with an iron fist and no one was allowed to make mistakes! Jamie took out the photo, "This here is Satch. He lives in a box over there," he pointed, "and he's been around here for ages. We ain't seen him for a long time, so we think he might have fucked off."

"Who are his friends?"

Freddy looked around, "That guy with the guitar over there and," he paused, "I'm lookin' for Kylie. She has the box next to his but I don't see her. Ah, and that black kid over there, Franklin; he knows Satch real well."

Wilf stood and walked towards the black kid, "Come here, Franklin," he said, when he got up to him. The kid made to run away. "Don't!" Wilf said.

"What do you need, boss?" He was terrified! He knew who Wilf was!

"I need you, to tell me where Satch is."

"Satch? Oh, he's gone, man. He ain't here no more."

"Where'd he go?"

"He got a flat, over near Brixton."

"You know where it is?"

"Yep, I do. I followed him there, one time. They got a whore house next door to it. Some Albanian guys. Real mean fuckers! People traffickers, you know! Very dangerous! I think Satch has been workin' for them. I heard, he was stealin' babies for them."

"People traffickers, huh."

"Yep, they are. Tough fuckers, them guys!"

"Right, well, you stay right here. You'll be comin' with us, to show me Satch's flat."

"OK, boss." He were more terrified than ever, now!

Wilf went back to Jamie and Freddy, "Give me that bag, Jules." Jules handed him the gym bag he had with him. Wilf unzipped it and let them look inside. There was £20,000 and half a kilo of heroin inside! "You guys done good! From now on, if you need anything, you call me directly! You just moved up! I don't often say it, but thanks a lot! You've helped me and I look kindly on anyone that does that!" He held out his hand and they both shook it. They were beaming. "Let's go, Jules." Jules stood up. Freddy and Jamie, high fived each other! They were delighted!

As they were walking back to the car, Wilf motioned with his head for Franklin to follow them. "Call Harris, Jules and tell him to get two more guys and let me know when he's ready. I'll tell him where to meet us, after this Franklin kid shows me where Satch's flat is. He said, it's near Brixton."

"Sure, OK boss." He dialed.

They got into the car and Wilf said, "OK, Franklin, which way is it, boy?"

"Turn left here and in three streets, turn right, then go straight." They drove for half an hour, with Franklin giving directions and he, finally said, "OK, stop here. You see that blue door?" Wilf nodded. "Well, that's it. Not sure what flat he lives in but it's in there somewhere."

Wilf took out a big wad of money. He peeled off five £50 notes and handed them to him, "You done good, kid. You're gonna walk back, OK?"

Franklin wanted to run! He took the money and said, "OK, yeah, thanks boss!" He got out of the car and then, he did run!

"Call Harris and tell him where we are, Jules. He's from Brixton, so he'll know it." They sat, watching the blue door. It was evening and the sun was going down. Men went into the blue door and then came out. "It's a whore house, alright," Wilf said. "Busy one, by the looks of it."

Some time later, Harris appeared with two other guys. They got into the car. "Hey boss, what's up?"

"You armed?" Harris nodded. "Good, you see that blue door?" A man was coming out of it. "In there, somewhere, is the flat of the guy that took David. A kid told us, there's an Albanian whore house in there too. He said that they're people traffickers, so I'm guessin' that, probably this Satch guy took my son for them to sell him. We're gonna have to go in very heavy, 'cause these Albanians are usually pretty well ready, for just about anything! Let's go!"

They all got out of the car and went to the blue door. Inside, they found the stairs with two doors, one on either side of the landing. They went, quietly up the stairs and Wilf stopped in front of the doors. The one on the right, opened and a man came out of it. They could hear music, inside and when the door was all the way open, Wilf, followed by the others, guns drawn, rushed inside!

They saw the half naked women and children and their clients and Gjin was there. He was sitting on the sofa drinking a beer, with a naked little girl on his lap. He was almost drunk. When he saw the unwanted visitors, he jumped to his feet, knocking the girl onto the floor and he roared! Wilf hit him on the side of his head with his pistol and he went down! Everyone started screaming! Unusually, Lorik was there! He liked one of the girls, so he had, lately, become a regular visitor to the place. When he heard Gjin roar and the girls scream, he ran, naked out of the room he was in and was confronted by four, armed black guys who were all staring at him!

He put his hands above his head! Wilf looked at Gjin, "Tie that fucker up, Jules!" Jules tore the phone cable out of the wall, smacked Gjin in the mouth and tied his hands behind his back. Wilf looked at Lorik, "You, get on your knees and keep your hands up. Everyone else, get into those bedrooms and stay there!" Terrified, the girls ran out of the room! He looked at Sasha, "Where's Satch?"

Sasha snarled at him, "Fuck off!" Wilf smacked her and she fell to the floor! She laughed, "You cannot hurt me!"

Wilf went over to Lorik, "Is that Satch's flat, across the landing?" Lorik nodded. "Where is he?" Lorik shook his head. "Jules, kick that door down!

We're gonna use that flat to find out from these fuckers, where Satch and my baby boy are!"

Jules went out of the flat and with one kick, the door to the other flat was open; the door was wrecked! Gjin, Sasha and Lorik were dragged into it. When they were all inside, Wilf said, "Harris, go down to the car and bring the tool box up here. I gotta ask these fuckers some questions." Harris laughed and went out.

When he returned, he opened the tool box and put it next to Wilf. Wilf took a battery operated drill out of it and sat on the floor next to Gjin, who was bleeding, heavily from his mouth. "Now," he said, "I'm gonna ask, each of you, two questions. First," he looked at each of them, "where is Satch? Second, where is my son? Two simple questions. And, each time you refuse to answer, I'm gonna start to drill! Toes first and then I'll work my way up and believe me, when I say, that, I've done this before and I know exactly how to do it, to get the best effect!" He looked at Gjin, "You first! Question one!" Gjin didn't speak; just shook his head. His head and mouth were bleeding, heavily. "Hold him guys!" Two guys held him and Wilf grabbed his right foot, put the drill bit against Gjin's big toe and pulled the trigger. Gjin started to scream and the blood gushed out of his foot! "Question two!" Gjin was sobbing but he shook his head! He grabbed the other foot and did the same thing on his other big toe! Gjin screamed again!

Sasha wet herself! She was terrified! "Now, you bitch! You told me to fuck off!" He grabbed her left ankle and pushed the drill bit into her foot! She screamed and fainted!

Wilf looked at Lorik, "Now you, big man! On you, I'm gonna start on your knee! First question!" He raised the drill and placed the bit on Lorik's knee and the guys grabbed his shoulders.

"He is in Portugal."

"Second question!"

"Flutura has your son. She was going to sell him for a lot of money but when she found out, he is your son, she decided to keep him. She was going to call you, to return him. She does not want any trouble with you!" Gjin started yelling something in Albanian and Jules smashed him on top of his head!

He fell over, unconscious!

"Now, you see how easy that was?" He handed his mobile to Lorik, "Call her, now!"

Lorik dialed a number and said something in his language and handed the phone to Wilf. He said, "You'll take my son to Brixton Tube Station, right now." He closed the phone and turned to Lorik. "You done good." He took a pen and paper out of his pocket and handed it to him. "Write down, where Satch is, in Portugal." Lorik took the pen and paper and wrote something and handed the paper to Wilf. "Good, now that was easy, wasn't it!" He looked at his team. "Let's go pick up my son, guys."

They waited at the tube station for twenty minutes. A limousine came up and a well dressed man got out of it, carrying a baby in a red blanket. They could see a woman inside it. The man handed the baby to Jules and got back into the car. It pulled away from the curb and was gone. The baby was sleeping.

Escape

I went back to the house and about 10:00, the house was full of clients. I was lying on my bed, watching a film when I heard a gun shot! Very loud! Then, the screaming and shouting started. I heard, "Where is the fucker?" Another gun shot and then I heard Fatos shouting at Anibal, to get down!

Elena burst into my room! She was dressed in a light blue dress and she was wearing sandals. She ran up to me, "These men want you, Satch! Four big black guys! They have guns!" Another two shots and I heard Fatos yelling!

I grabbed my pack with the money in it, my passport and Elena's passport and then I locked the door and said, "Now, stay here, quiet with me. Don't move!"

We could hear the commotion, downstairs

and I went to look over the balcony. I saw one guy, holding a gun, standing near the pool and I could hear the others shouting at Anibal, "We know he's here, Anibal, now bring him here or we're gonna kill everybody!" Anibal said something but I couldn't hear the words.

I went to Elena, "Now, listen to me, babe. We're gonna go down the corridor and down the stairs that the servants use. We can get out the back way, without being seen. I've got your passport, so let's go, nice and easy, OK?"

She was trembling but she nodded and got to her feet. "OK," she said, "I will follow you."

I slowly, opened the door and I could hear the little ones, crying, downstairs. We crept along the corridor to the stairs and we, very quietly went down them. There was a door at the bottom and I opened it and we went out of it and then ran for all we were worth! We ran into the town and I saw the homeless people. The German was there, "We need to go, now!" I said to him.

They'd heard the gunshots, "You, from over there?" I nodded. "OK, brother, you're here with us, now! You and Joana get inside Ramon's tent. You'll be OK in there." We slid into the tent and I could see that Elena was wide eyed and shaking with fear!

I put my arms around her and helped her to the floor of the tent. "We're OK, now. These people will help us!"

The German came into the tent. "Your ride will be here in 15 minutes. You got the cash?"

I reached into my pack and took out a big wad of money; all £50 notes. I peeled off £1000 for him and then I said, "£200, each, for everyone else. All they have to do is stay quiet." £1200 more! Worth it!

He nodded and smiled, "Quiet, they will be! We are, all brothers, no?" I gave him the cash and he went out.

Our ride, an old farm truck with goats in the back, stopped next to the square. "OK, this it, my friend. Jose will take you to the harbour in Viana do Castelo and you will get into a sailboat. The man on the boat, Filipe will take you wherever you want to go. Another £1000 for him, yes?" I nodded. "OK, go well, my English friend!"

We ran to the truck and jumped into the back with the goats. As soon as we were onboard, the driver pulled away, fast. We went through the night, down some pretty rough roads for about an hour. I could smell the sea. I had no idea what or where Viana do Castelo was, but hopefully it would be safe for us. Elena wasn't doing very well. She was trembling and she said, "Oh my, Satch, are we going to be killed? I am very worried!"

"Well, I hope not, love! We just have to trust these guys!"

A short time later, the truck stopped and Jose opened the flap. "Vamos, estamos aqui!" (Let's go! We're here!) What? He held out his hand and I put £500 into it. He smiled.

Elena said, "Obrigada, (thank you) senor! Vamos!" (Let's go!) Of course, she could speak Portuguese, couldn't she!

He led us to a small marina and there was a tall, dark haired man with a very dark tan, about 50 years old and standing next to him was a short, dark haired woman. He said, "You, our passengers?" American accent.

I smiled at him and said, "Yep, we're them! Felipe?" He nodded.

He held out his hand, "You got somethin' for me?" I handed him £1000 and he nodded at the woman, "OK, let's get movin' then!"

At the house, Wilf, Jules and his guys had everyone lined up, against the wall. They were pointing guns at them and Anibal said, "Please, gentlemen, you may search the house but this person you are looking for, is not here. We run a very good, clean business and we do not participate in anything that will hurt us."

Wilf stepped forward, "Look, mate, we've been told that this Satch guy is here. It was your own people in London that told us that! Now," he held the gun against Anibal's head, "where is he?"

Anibal held up his hands, "As I said, please search the house." He looked at Fatos, "Take them around the house, Fatos. Show them that this person is not here!" He had noticed that Elena was missing.

Fatos moved forward with his hands up, "Will you follow me, please?" They'd taken his weapon but he wasn't afraid of them! He'd fought in wars and been with the Albanians since he was a boy. He had his own ideas about black people!

He led Jules, Harris and one other guy, around the house. They went room to room, while Wilf stayed with Anibal and the girls. The young ones were sitting on the floor in tears. "Asha whispered to her friend, Anita, "I hope they don't find Satch!" Anita took her hand, nodded and cried, quietly.

After an hour of searching, They came down the stairs, "Nothin' boss. He ain't here."

Wilf said, "That fucker in London lied to us!" He looked at Asha and walked over to her. She cowered away from him! He crouched down and he could see all the bruises on her little body. He looked into her eyes; they were full of tears and she was terrified! "Where's Satch?" he said, in a very low voice. Asha started talking, very quickly and excitedly in her own language – Lithuanian! Wilf couldn't understand a word of what she was saying, except the word Satch a few times! She kept pointing at the swimming pool and then she burst into tears! Wilf stood and shook his head. "Fuck!" he shouted. "Let's get the fuck out of here!" Asha looked at Anibal and he nodded and smiled at her! She could speak English, perfectly when she wanted to!

We climbed aboard the sailboat, a very nice one and sat in the cockpit. The woman untied the ropes, holding it to the dock. "All set!" she said.

He started the engine and we were off! When we got out of the marina, he said, "OK, honey, let's get those sails up."

The woman went to the bow and unfurled a large sail and then she went to help him to put the mainsail up. It was a very warm, starry night and as we got into the ocean, further, I could feel the breeze getting stronger and the waves lifting the boat. The sails filled and Filipe turned the boat, so that the wind pushed us along. Elena was holding my arm, tightly and when I looked at her, she smiled. I kissed her cheek, "We're OK, now, my love." I said to her.

When we were underway, the woman sat next to Elena and held out her hand, "Tina," she said. Portuguese accent.

Elena shook her hand, "Elena, and this is Satch." Tina shook my hand, too.

Filipe came to sit with us, "She's on auto now," he said. He looked at me, "Where do you want go?"

I smiled, "I have no idea! You got any suggestions?"

He laughed, "All I was told, is that you guys needed a ride and £1000 buys you a nice, long trip, so all you gotta do now, is tell me where we're goin'.

It's a very big ocean!"

I looked at Elena. She shrugged. I wasn't sure how much I should tell this guy. "Well, we need to go somewhere where we can be off grid for a while."

"Corvo!" they said together.

"Corvo?" I said, puzzled.

Filipe, laughed again and looked at Tina, "Yes, Corvo! It's a little island in the Azores, about 1000 nautical miles from here. We can sail there, in around 6 or 7 days. It's a nice journey, at this time of year. We get a good north west wind and the current is goin' in the right direction. It's got a little village called, Vila do Corvo with about 500 people livin' there. Nice little place. Lots of tourists, now and there's some nice little places to stay, that don't cost a lot. They got phones and internet, too if you need it."

I hugged Elena a little tighter, "What do you say, babe?"

She smiled, "Sounds good!"

"OK, Corvo, it is, Filipe!"

He stood up, "Good! I'll set our course and

would you guys like beer or some nice, Portuguese port wine?"

I let go of Elena, "I'd like a beer."

Elena said, "Wine for me, please!"

Tina stood up, "Great! I'll get drinks for all of us!" They went below, together.

I turned and looked at the lights, onshore. They were getting smaller, as we went out to sea and I thought about the chaos we had left behind at the house. Did those people have a reach that would go all the way to Corvo? I looked at Elena; she looked very worried. I said, "Well, here we go, babe. These, seem like good people, so hopefully we'll be safe."

"This is the first time, in ten years that I have not been in their control," she said. "They will look everywhere for me and if they find me, I will be sent to Romania for sure!" She was almost crying!

I kissed her and took her hand, "Anibal told me that they were sending you to Romania, any day now."

She looked shocked, "He said, that?"

"Yes, he said that you are too old, now and

the clients, want, only young ones."

She started crying, quietly. I hugged her, tightly. Tina came up with drinks for us. She saw Elena crying and then she sat next to her, "Do not worry, Senora, you are good here. Filipe will never let anything happen to us. He is a strong man!" She handed the drinks to us and I drained my beer in one go! She smiled, "I will get you, another." She went below.

Filipe came up, carrying a beer and he had one for me, "Here you go, buddy." He looked at Elena, "I don't know and I don't wanna to know why you're here, Satch but while you are here, you're gonna be OK; I can guarantee it!" He touched his beer can to mine, "Drink up, sport! We got lots more!" I sat, sipping my beer and Elena drank some of her wine. I started to relax. I looked back at the shore and I could hardy see the lights, now.

Tina came back on deck, "I have put some food on for us. We will eat a nice meal and then I will show you, your cabin." We sat drinking our drinks and I could feel Elena starting to relax.

I'd never been on a sailboat, so the feeling

was strange but very enjoyable. The boat was going through the water, silently, heeling slightly and the movement was very smooth. I looked around me and all I could see was the black sky, filled with stars and the black water.

We went below to a very nice, brightly lit salon with a U shaped, red velvet sofa and a small kitchen. All chrome and very neat. We ate a good Portuguese stew; Jardineira, Tina called it. We ate Portuguese bread and drank just enough red wine to finally start to feel normal. Elena, still looked shaken and I was sure, that after she got some sleep, she would be better. While we were eating, Filipe said, "You done much sailin', Satch?"

I laughed, "I've never been on a sailboat before, Filipe! This is a first for me!" I sipped, the very good wine. "I've been on a lot of canal boats in London but nothing like this."

He looked at Elena, "And how about you, young lady?"

Elena smiled, "Yes, I used to sail every day, on the Adriatic when I was a child. Nothing like this boat, of course but my father, once told me that, if you can sail a small boat, you can sail a big one, no?"

"That's right! This is a 46 footer and she's as easy to sail as a dinghy! And where did you sail in the Adriatic?"

"I am, originally from Budva but I have not seen it for many years."

He looked at Tina and smiled, "Why, we know Budva very well, don't we, honey! Me and Tina used to run a charter boat in that part of the world! Nice place! Lots of tourists and nice beaches!" Tina nodded.

"So, you know Gospostina, also?"

Tina laughed! "Ah, yes, we know it! It is a good place to eat and drink, no?"

Elena sat up a bit straighter and smiled! "Yes, this is true! My father had a small café there! He lost it, due to his gambling debts but we always enjoyed going there!"

"How about some nice Portuguese brandy?" Filipe said.

I nodded and Elena said, "Oh no, not for me! I need to sleep!"

Filipe stood up and went to a small bar with bottles on it and he looked at me, "Well, I know Tina won't drink brandy, so it's just you and me, sport! Let's let the ladies do the cleanin' up and we'll go up top and drink this nectar, OK?" I stood up, took the snifter he handed me and then I went up to the cockpit.

When we were seated, I could see that the lights on shore were no longer visible. Filipe said, "I can see that your girl has been through some shit, Satch." I was about to speak and he held his hand up, "It's OK! Me and Tina has seen some serious shit around Europe, so you got no problems with us. Like I said, earlier, I don't really want to know what's happened for you to be with us but if you want to talk about it, feel free. It's up to you."

I looked at him and I could hear Elena and Tina, below, chatting in Portuguese. "Well, for now, I think, the less you know, the better it is for you."

He sipped his brandy and looked at me, over the rim of the glass, "That bad, huh?" I nodded. No more talk and we sat there with the stars shining on us.

A short time later, Elena called up, "Bed time, Satch!"

I looked at Filipe and smiled. "That means goodnight, Filipe!" I said, finishing the brandy.

"Have a good one."

I went below and Elena led me to a cabin in the bow. It had a big, soft bed and its own toilet room. I undressed and when I looked at Elena, she was, already asleep. I used the toilet, laid on the bed and I was asleep in two seconds! I'd spent some time on canal boats on the London canals. A lot of people live on those boats and some of them are very nice to the homeless. I'd sit, getting high on marijuana and drinking beer with them and have a really good time! This sailboat was something else! When I woke up, I could feel the boat being lifted by the waves and I could hear, the hissing as the bow went through the water. It felt great! I didn't want to get up! I rolled over, next to Elena and put my arm around her. She moaned a bit and then put her arms around me, "Oh Satch, what will we do now?" She was crying, again. "I am so worried that they will find us!"

I held her tightly, "Let's take it, one step at a time, honey. Let's get to this Corvo place and then see what's next." We sailed, steadily in excellent weather and Filipe, quickly showed me how to move the sails and as we were on autopilot, there was no need to steer.

On the sixth morning, after a nice breakfast, just as we were getting used to being on the boat, Filipe yelled, "Land ho!" startling us! We, all looked where he pointed and I could just see a dim shadow on the horizon. Ilha do Corvo!

"There's not really, any good places to anchor in this place," Filipe said, "but there is a small dock and we'll drop you guys there. There's a few good B&Bs and rooms for rent, so you should be OK, there. The food and wine is real good and the people will let you keep to yourselves. They see tourists all the time."

Elena had been looking at the island as it grew larger, "Are there any prostitutes there?"

"Prostitutes?"

She nodded, "Yes, prostitutes."

Filipe looked at Tina, shrugged and laughed,

"Well, I got no idea, on that one! There's only, around 500 people that live there, so I'm sure there might be some but if there are, it's probably not an organised thing or anything!" He looked puzzled.

Elena wasn't looking at anyone, "Well, we will see, I am sure." She shook her head. She was watching the land come closer. I could see how nervous she was.

We arrived in Corvo, four hours later. The sea was rough and as we tied up at the small dock, the boat was being lifted very high by the waves. "OK, you guys," Filipe said, "we're gonna have to leave you here! We're on our way to the Canaries, so we can't stay here long." He held out his hand to me, "It was good knowin' you, Satch!" He touched Elena's cheek and smiled at her. He patted his shirt pocket, "And thanks for the cash!" I shook his hand.

Tina kissed me on both cheeks and she gave Elena a big hug, "You'll be OK, menina! (girl). Do not worry! You have a good man!"

We got out of the boat and my legs wobbled when I stood on the dock! Elena leaned against me and laughed! I said, "Thanks for the ride, Filipe!

Hopefully, we'll meet again, some day!" He nodded and smiled.

He switched on the engine and Tina untied the lines. They waved to us, as they backed away from the dock. We watched them put the sails up and sail away.

In Penafiel, Sr. Costa had to make a phone call, that he did not want to make. Elena had run away with Satch and he had to tell his superiors in Lisboa about it. Any escapee had to be reported, immediately, so that the searchers could be mobilised. It would reflect badly on him! "Ah, Marco, this is Anibal. How are you, amigo?"

"Anibal, what a nice surprise! How is your family doing?" Of course he meant the girls in Anibal's house.

"We have a small problem here, Marco."

Marco knew what he meant, "Which one is it?"

"Elena."

"Elena!"

"Yes, she has gone away with, Satch, the man from London."

"Ah, Anibal, this is not good. When did she go?"

"She went, last night. We had a visit from some black men from London, that came here to look for Satch. They were armed and they caused a big disturbance. Fortunately, no one was seriously hurt. It will affect our business, here, for a few days but then we will go back to normal."

Silence. Anibal waited, nervously. Finally, "Well, amigo, I will tell Tirana and they will start the search. I have her photo but I will need one of Satch. I'm sure you have one?"

"Yes, yes, of course I do."

"Good, well, send that to me today."

"This will not go well for her and Satch, that is sure, as you know. You have had a very good record up to now, so nothing will come to you but, now, Tirana will be watching you, a bit more closely. I'm sure you do not want to go to Romania, do you."

"No, no, I do not."

"Good, so for now, let us continue as we have been doing. Your profits are up and I know that, you always do things the right way. Let's, let this thing pass and we will continue, as usual, yes?"

"Yes, that is best."

"Good, then, I will speak to you soon, my friend."

When Anibal put the phone down, he was sweating! That, Marco had said the word Romania to him, had him wanting to run away! He knew what that meant! He had always been a loyal worker for the family but he knew that that could change in a second!

Marco put the phone down and opened his computer. He found Elena's photo and sent it, in an email to Tirana. He knew that they would, immediately, alert the search team. He smiled, as he sent it, imagining how quickly they would contact everyone in the Portuguese and other European governments. The family had contacts everywhere, with everyone of any importance! Elena had no chance as long as she was in Europe! He knew of this Satch person and he smiled, again as he thought of him being in one of their special houses in Romania. The death houses!

The email that Marco sent was received by Blinera Kurti. She was the leader of the search team in Tirana. She sat, looking at the photo of Elena and sighed. Why did these young women think they could get away? She went into the database and found Elena. She saw that the girl had run twice before when she was much younger and that she was scheduled to be sent to Romania the following week. And this Satch person, the baby thief from London had gone with her! She had his photo, as well and she smiled when she looked at it. He was a nice looking, young man! She shook her head; two more for Romania when they were caught! She sent the details to the search team in Portugal and to the people in Montenegro, in case they would have to visit Elena's family, then, she went onto other work.

Reynaldo, in Lisboa received the message from Blinera. He laughed when he read the details! An Englishman! He was used to searching for runaway girls, so looking for an Englishman would be interesting! "Hey, Alfredo, look at this!"

Alfredo was his colleague, "What is it, Rey?"

"We have an Englishman, a baby thief!"

"An Englishman!"

"Yes, look at this. He has taken one of the girls from Sr. Anibal in Penafiel!"

"Filho da puta! (son of a bitch)!" He looked at Elena's photo and laughed, "Well, she is not a baby, is she?"

Reynaldo smiled, "No, my friend, she is not! We will enjoy this one before we send her to Romania, no?" They always used and abused the girls and women when they found them! They knew what their destiny was, once found. "So, let's get to work!

Clues

After viewing the CCTV footage of the homeless people, George Mason and Liz went to the taped off area in King's Cross. The forensic people were inside the boxes looking for evidence and he knew that he'd have to wait, to see what they found. There was a team of police, interviewing homeless people, to find out where Morty had gone. Of course, everyone said the same thing – they didn't know where he was. George knew that the homeless world was a closed place and that anyone that wasn't part of it, wasn't part of it. He knew that they were cautious and suspicious of anyone that tried to intrude into their world; especially the police!

He called his team together, "Well, let's start to round up some of these people," he said. "We'll take them to our place for questioning. Someone, probably a lot of people, know who this kidnapper is and we need to find out what they know. If we make their life difficult enough, someone'll tell us who he is. We've got a name; Satch. We'll start with that."

When they got back to their task force office, Liz went to her computer and opened the national database, ViCLAS (Violent Crime Linkage Analysis System), and typed in the name Satch. Nothing came back. She frowned at the screen and said to George, "This guy's, gotta have another name."

"Yes, he probably does, but we won't know what it is, until one of these people tell us something." He looked at the gathered group from the canal and watched as they were questioned by the team. He went into an interview room and started to ask a young woman questions. Who is Satch? Does she know him? Where is he now? Questions. She said, she knew nothing and who is Satch?

Finally, one of the constables came out of an interview room with a name, "Simon Atcheson." He'd been interviewing a young prostitute and she had given him the name!

Liz typed the name into the database and, yes, he'd been arrested for shoplifting, when he was younger and they had his details on file, including his photo. She sat looking at him and laughed, "How does a guy like this, a shoplifter, get into stealing babies?" The rest of the team came over to her and looked at her monitor.

"That's him, alright," George said. "Now, where is he?"

Liz looked through the record, "A couple of warnings for shoplifting, a juvenile record; no known affiliates in the people trafficking world. I don't get it!"

Another constable came out of an interview room, "I got a guy, here, says that Satch left his box some time ago and got a flat. He says he knows where the flat is."

"Bring him out here," George said. The constable brought the guy out. George looked at him; young, scruffy, needed a bath. "What's your name?"

"Luke Jacobs."

"So, Luke, how do you know about this flat?"

Luke smiled, "I don't know nothin' about it. Me and my friend followed Satch to there, one day."

"Where is it?"

"Near, Brixton Tube Station."

"What's the address?"

Luke laughed, "I don't know the address, mate! I know where it is though. There's a whore house, next door, run by them Albanians. We left quick like, 'cause they's very dangerous people! Somehow, Satch got involved with them! He's probably dead or workin' in one of their places, suckin' cocks! They're really dangerous, you know! They take homeless people and kill them! Everyone knows it!" George looked at Liz and she shook her head.

"Can you take us to it?"

Luke, looked afraid, "Don't know, man. I don't want them to know, I told you about the flat. They'll put me in one of their snuff films!"

"Don't worry about that. We'll just drive past it and you can point it out to us. After that, we'll take you back to the canal, OK?"

Luke, very reluctantly, nodded, yes. "OK, but you gotta make sure, they don't know, I told you!"

"Don't worry, they won't know." He looked at Liz, "Let's go."

They got into an unmarked car and Luke gave them directions. When they got there, "OK, you see that blue door?" George nodded. "That's the place. If you just sit here for a few minutes, you'll see the men go in and out. Ah, look, see, there goes a guy now." The watched a man go into the blue door and a short time later, one came out of it. "A whore house, like I said, you see?" He slumped down, deeper into the seat. "OK, you know where it is. Can we go now?" As he said it, another man went into the door and another came out. George drove back to the canal, let Luke out and he ran away, as fast as he could!

"So, all we have to do, is get a search warrant and I think we might know a lot more about our Satch fellow."

When George went into the task force room, he was called by Billy. "Come in here for a second, George."

George went into Billy's office, "What's up?"

"One of the homeless guys, said that one of the babies that Satch, snatched, was the son of Wilf Sutton."

George sat in a chair, "We know about that. That's bad news."

"Yeah, it is."

"Well, I guess we have to work around that, too."

"The guy said that Wilf is looking for Satch, too. You know what's gonna happen, if he finds him, first."

George smiled, "Yeah, I know exactly what's going to happen." He didn't say that they had given the photos of Satch, to Sally.

"OK, well, I wanted to let you know."

"Good, we'll have the search warrant for that flat, later today and then we'll go there and have a look around."

"OK, good one."

George went back to his desk and an hour later, Liz came over to him, holding a slip of paper. "What's up?" he asked.

"Satch's flat? We got the search warrant."

"Yeah!"

"There was a home invasion, there, an hour ago and people got hurt!"

George jumped to his feet! "Shit, let's get over there!" He drove fast, to the flat and when they got there, they could see the flashing blue and red lights and there was a crowd of people gathered around. The area was taped off and when they got out of the car, they showed their badges and went inside and up the stairs. George looked around the flat. There was blood everywhere! He looked at the detective next to him, "Who got hurt?"

"Some of the people in the flat across the

landing. They're not talking. One of the punters called us. He wouldn't leave his name when he called. These people don't want us here, so they're not saying anything, either, but it's pretty messy."

George and Liz went into the flat, across the landing and found Gjin, Sasha and Lorik sitting at the kitchen table. The paramedics had bandaged Gjin's head and his feet and Sasha had a big bandage around her head and her left foot, too. George looked at Lorik. He was dressed in a bath robe and looking out the window. "So, what's your name?"

Lorik looked at him, "My name is Lorik."

"What happened here, Lorik?"

"I don't know. I came here to visit my friends and some black guys came here and did all of this."

George sighed and nodded, knowingly; he looked around the room and saw a female officer with a group of young girls, about 12 years old. "And who are those young girls?"

Lorik looked at them. His favourite, Lucy, was there. "I have no idea. I have never seen them before."

Sasha was sitting up straight, frowning. She

had dried blood on her face. "And you, what's your name?" George asked.

"I am not speaking." She looked out the window.

Gjin moaned. "Are you going to say anything?" George asked. Gjin shook his head and groaned again, rubbing his left foot.

George stood, "OK, let's get them down to the station. We'll talk to them, there." He looked at Gjin, "Do you know, Satch?" Gjin looked away from him.

Liz went to the female officer that was talking to the children, "Hi, I'm DC Liz Dawson, what do we have here?"

"Hi Liz, I'm DC Lily Charlton. I work the prostitution and sex slave unit. We've got a group of young girls here, that have been working as prostitutes for these people. Two of them are from France, one is Spanish and the other one is from Manchester. They're terrified to say anything! It's going to take some time to find out any details. We're going to take them to a shelter and I'm sure we'll get the whole story, but they're all, really afraid to speak. I've seen this before, of course." She looked at the others, "They look, Albanian. We've got a big crew of them in the UK, running this people trafficking thing. Always using these little girls in their business. The girls won't know much of the details but whatever they can tell us, will help us."

"OK, Lily, thanks for that." She looked at the girls. "You'll be alright girls, don't worry." The girls, two of them, quietly crying and shaking, were not looking at her, they were looking at Sasha with fear in their eyes! She was looking at them, too!

She went back to George, "Looks like this is under control, George. We might as well go and look at that flat and see if Satch left anything behind."

Safety

Now what? We had our small bags with us and we were standing on the dock with big waves hitting it! We walked into the town and saw that it had an airport and not much else. We got into the centre of the town, in less than an hour and saw the Hotel Comodoro.

We went inside and were met by a smiling

man in a white shirt, "Bom dia, good morning!" he said, smiling.

I smiled at him, "Do you have any rooms?"

"Yes, of course we do, sir. We have some very nice rooms here. For how long will you stay?"

"Two weeks."

"Ah, very nice, two weeks is good! You will enjoy it here! Please sign the book and show me your passports, please." I got out my passport, signed the book and Elena showed him, hers. He handed me a key. "Just out and to the right, sir; room 11. Continental breakfast is available from 7:00 to 10:00 every morning. Please enjoy your stay, here."

I had signed in, as Norman Johnson from New York City and, if he noticed the different name on my passport, he didn't say anything to me about it. We went to the room and fell onto the bed. Elena held me tightly, "Oh Satch! I hope we are good now!" I held her and we fell asleep.

When we woke up, it was early evening! We'd been asleep for almost five hours! I kissed Elena and sat up. I could hear a plane landing at the airport which was a short distance away. Elena stirred, snuggled closer to me and kissed me. We lay there for a while and then we got up and sat at the small table, in the room. "Let's go and get some food, my love and take a look at this place. We're going to be here, for, at least, the next two weeks, so let's go and see where we are."

We stood up, washed and went into the town. Elena was looking at everyone. "Why are you looking at everyone, so closely, Elena?" I asked.

"Because I know their look! I know everything about those people and I am seeing if they are here, like they are, everywhere else in Europe! I will know them, man or woman when I see them!"

We walked for some time and then we saw a small restaurant. Just the kind of place, one would eat at! As we went inside, I stopped, "Elena, you know what? I, only have £50 notes. No Euros!"

She took my hand and smiled, "These people will be very happy to exchange your English money for Euros! It is the same, everywhere in Europe!"

We sat at a table and a pretty, teenaged girl

came over with menus. "Boa tarde, good afternoon, here is our menu."

"Thank you," I said, "we would like a bottle of red wine, please." I took a £50 note out of my wallet and showed it to her, "Will you accept English money, here?"

She smiled, "Sim, yes, of course we do, sir. My father will exchange it for you!" She pointed at a sign that said, Cambio. "This is an exchange bureau, as you can see."

I took out £200 and handed it to her, "Could you give us Euros for this?"

She took the cash, "Of course, sir, I will do that."

Elena smiled, "You see? Europe!"

The girl returned with a handful of cash, "250 Euros, sir."

"Thank you." We ordered fish with potatoes and salad and drank the wine. It was excellent food!

We went back to the room and sat at the table. "So, now we are here," Elena said. "I did not see any of them, yet and no prostitutes in the street, so maybe we are OK. We will go out again, tomorrow and see if they are here."

I put my hand on hers, "I think we're safe, love."

"We will see." We went for a short walk and then, to bed and to sleep.

"I woke up, early in the morning and got up and made a cup of tea. I sat, looking out the window, thinking; 'Now what? We can't stay here forever. At some point we have to go. To where'? I was sure that Elena, with all of her travel experience would be able to come up with some good places to go. Money was no problem and we had our passports.

She woke up and we took a shower together. As we soaped each other, we kissed and soaking wet, we fell on the bed and made love! Sex with her was intense! She really liked it and I really enjoyed feeling her come alive!

Afterwards, we lay side by side. "And now, Satch. What do we do now?"

I held her close to me, "Something; I just don't know what, yet. We can't stay here forever."

She rolled onto her side and propped her

head up with her hand and looked at me. "You are right, there."

"I was hoping that you would have some good ideas about where to go."

She laughed and put her hand on my chest, "I do, actually, have some very good ideas. I have been thinking about this for many, many years! When men are fucking me, I think about it, all the time! It helps me, to do it with them! I know of two girls, that also, have escaped and I know their telephone numbers. One of them is in Turkey and the other is in Mozambique. The Albanians do not go to those places. If we can get a mobile phone, I can telephone them."

"We'll get one, today."

She rolled against me, put her hand on my penis, smiled and said, "One more time, please!" We made love, again! Very nice!

We had a breakfast on the terrace at a little café and Elena, constantly watched everyone. She put her hand on my arm, smiled and said, "They are not here."

We found a small shop that had mobile

phones in the window. I bought two of them with SIM cards and we went and sat on the small beach. Elena called her friend, Ajola, in Turkey. "She is from my country," she said. She spoke for some time in a language, I didn't know and then, she said, "We may go to Turkey. My friend said that they are not there. She has a family and she told me that her family is safe. I asked her to check on my family and she said, that I should call her, at this time, tomorrow. She will check on them for me."

She dialed the number for her other friend in Mozambique. Again, she spoke in her own language and then she said, "My friend said that Mozambique is unsafe now because of the terrorists but the Albanians are not there. The business, is all being done by local Mafia and the Chinese are there, financing everything. She advises that we do not go there." She handed me the phone.

"Well, OK, I'll call my friend and see if she knows what's happening in London." I dialed Milton's number. Kylie did not and would not have a mobile phone. He answered, "Milton! It's Satch!"

"Satch; fuck man! You're in deep shit! Where

you callin' from? No, don't tell me! The Bill's, everywhere, lookin' for you, man! Stealin' babies or some shit and Wilf and them drug dealers wants you, too!"

"Is Kylie with you?"

I heard a rustling sound, then, "Oh you fuckin' idiot!" Kylie! "What the fuck have you done? They're lookin' for you, everywhere! There's no fuckin' peace at all, here because of it! They've picked up everyone, includin' me and Milton and everyone else, askin' us questions about you! Don't tell me where you are; just don't come anywhere near here! And on top of that, that Wilf Sutton's guys are everywhere, tryin' to find you, too! Did you really steal his fuckin' baby? Wilf's had all of the drugs taken out of King's Cross to try and force someone to tell them where you are! I can, hardly find anything when I need it! He's gonna take you to pieces, you know! And throw this fuckin' phone away; they might trace it!" She hung up.

I sat and watched the waves hit the beach. "I'm in big trouble!"

Elena touched my arm, "Why? What's

happened?"

"The cops are looking for me, everywhere and you know about the drug dealers!" I broke the phone in half, took out the SIM and threw the pieces into the ocean. Albanians, drug dealers and police looking for me and us!

We went for lunch at the same small restaurant, as the day before. We were sitting on the terrace, eating crab, rice and prawns. There were other people there and behind Elena, a couple came in with three children about 7-8 years old; two boys and a girl. The children were playing and laughing and then the man's phone rang. I couldn't understand what he was saying, because he was speaking a language I didn't know but when Elena heard him speak, she went white! "They're here!" she whispered. "He is Albanian! He is saying that he will watch out for someone! We must leave now!" She stood up and walked out of the terrace, towards the hotel.

I got up, paid the bill and ran after her. She was walking very fast! "We must get on a plane today, Satch! We must go, now!" She was almost running and tears were on her cheeks! She was terrified!

When we got to the room, I took her by the shoulders and led her to sit on the bed. I could feel her shaking. "Look," I said, "they don't know we're here. He could have been talking about anyone."

She held out her hand, "Give me money. I need to go! If you want to stay here, that is OK but I cannot take the chance! Do you not know what they will do to me if they find me! They will have a hundred men rape me before they torture and kill me! They will force the other girls to watch it! I have seen that happen to others! I must go, now, Satch, please!" She pushed me away with tears running down her cheeks and started to pack her small bag. I got up and did the same.

We walked to the airport, without telling the hotel we were leaving and when we got there, I looked up at the big board and saw that the next plane out, was going to Madrid. I bought two tickets and wondered how safe it would be. "We will not stay there, long," Elena said. "We must go to Turkey to meet, Ajola, my friend there."

As the plane took off, I thought about the next stop.

As we were descending for the landing, Elena became more and more worried. "They always have people at the airport, looking for new girls," she said. "They will see me, so you must hold my hand and act as if we are very close. Kiss me and show them that I am not alone. That will keep them away from us. I used to go with them to the airports to look for new girls, so I know how they work."

I said, "Well, that won't be too difficult, my little darling! We are very close!" She kissed me and I could feel her shaking.

"We will look for a flight to Turkey, today, if possible," she said. "We will stay in the airport."

When we landed, we went to the arrivals area and then, to the big board. There was a flight to Istanbul in three hours! I went and bought the tickets and Elena went into the toilet. "So, Elena, you are here in Madrid!"

She had just come out of a stall and she was startled! She turned and saw a young woman, with her arms crossed, smiling and leaning against the wall. "Marta! You are here?"

"Yes, Elena, I am here! They are looking for you, you know! And your pretty boyfriend! They want to take both of you, to Romania! There is a big reward for you!"

Elena was ready for a fight! "So, what do you need, Marta?" She clenched her fists! She was ready!

Marta put her hands in front of her. "No, no, Elena, Besart did not see you. Only I, saw you!"

"And now?"

"And now, you are safe! I remember how you helped me in Vienna, that time!" She was nodding, vigorously! "So, you are safe here! I will let your man know that you will stay here, in this room. Have you, a flight to catch?"

"Yes, in a little over two hours. We will need to get through security, so we have about one hour before I have to go there."

"Good, when Besart is not looking, I will tell your man what is happening." She went out and Elena slumped to the floor and cried!

I was sitting in a chair facing the toilet and when I saw the young woman leave the room, I waited for Elena but she didn't come out. I could see the big clock on the wall and as the hands moved, I wondered what had happened to her. Suddenly, the young woman I'd seen, came over to me and said, speaking very quietly, in heavily accented English, "Elena is hiding in the toilet room. You go to security and she will meet you there." She walked away. I'd almost jumped out of my chair when she spoke to me! Hiding? I watched the clock and as the time approached, I picked up my bag and went through security and sat at the departure gate for Istanbul and waited for Elena. What the Hell?

Almost an hour later, Elena came running up to me! "I am here! Let's go, onto the plane, quickly!"

We boarded the plane and as it took off, I said over and over, in my head, the words I'd heard a woman, saying, in the duty free shop – Mucho Bueno!

News

"A Simon Atcheson, boarded a plane in Corvo, in the Azores, bound for Madrid, yesterday afternoon and then he got on a flight to Istanbul!" Liz was smiling.

George had been squinting at his monitor, running down leads. He sat back in his chair and let out a long sigh. "Finally!"

Liz was beaming! "Yeah, the Turkish police have already been informed and they're on it."

"Well, hopefully, they'll nab him for us!"

Slowly, but surely the information on Simon (Satch) Atcheson was coming in. They found out who his parents were; a drug addict mother, now deceased and an alcoholic father, location unknown and they had run down most of his homeless friends, who were being as uncooperative as they could be.

The flat where the little girls were found had been fully searched, as had Satch's flat. Gjin, Sasha and Lorik had been arrested on multiple charges. The little girls had been taken by social services and none of them were talking. They were terrified! So far, Flutura and Guzim had not been mentioned.

"Any progress with those little girls?" George asked.

"Nope, they're not talking. They're very afraid! You know how this goes, though. They've probably been told that their families will be hurt, if they say anything. How many times have we seen this now? These bastards come to this country with their slaves and they think that's normal! Every time I hear about it, I want to scream!"

George shrugged, "I know." His phone rang, "Yeah? OK, sure." He put the phone down, "Billy wants to see us in his office."

They went into Billy's office and sat down, "You look tired, George! You, OK?"

George nodded and rubbed his face, "I am tired. I've been staring at that monitor for hours and I'm getting nowhere."

Billy held up a paper, "I've just spoken with a captain in the Turkish police. "Our boy landed in Istanbul from Madrid, this afternoon and he's got a young woman with him. They got through passport control before anyone knew about them. They've got the CCTV and it looks like they were picked up by a taxi and they went, straight into Istanbul. The Turks are trying to find out where they went. They're cooperating but I don't think it's any kind of priority for them. We'll have to wait and see if they get anything more."

"So, now we wait?" George said.

Billy nodded and smiled, "We wait. In the

meantime, let's get as much as we can from those little girls and the Albanians. I'm sure none of them will say much, but anything they can give us will be good."

Reynaldo got the same information as the British police, at the same time, about Satch and Elena, traveling to Turkey. He shook his head when he read that they were in Turkey. Off limits to his people! "Hey, Alfredo!"

"Sim, what is it?"

Rey smiled, "They are gone to Turkey!"

"Fuck!"

Turkey

My first thoughts of Istanbul was that it was chaos! The airport and everywhere else was noisy, dusty and crowded! It was very hot and humid! As soon as we stepped outside, we were attacked by taxi drivers; all wanting to take us somewhere! Which hotel? Do you need a room? Can I carry your bags? Noise, confusion! Elena's head was swiveling around, trying to see if anyone was watching us! She knew that they wouldn't be there but she was still afraid! We got into a taxi and when the driver asked me where we were going, I said, "Take us to a room that costs no more than 30 Euros per night."

"Ah, yes sir, you will go to my brother's hotel! You will like it very much! Do you have English money?" I nodded. "Ah, yes, well, this is much better than Euros. For this, my brother will give you good deal! He is good brother, sir!"

Elena was holding my arm, tightly. We watched Istanbul go past, as the sun went down. In a half an hour, we arrived at a small hotel. The driver said something to the man at reception and when I took two £50 notes out of my pocket, he bowed and winked at the driver, "This is very good, sir! You will have our best room. This money will buy you five nights in this excellent hotel!" He took the money and led us up the stairs to a very nice room.

When the door closed, Elena said, "Give me the phone and I will call my friend, to tell her we are here. I do not know where she is, in Turkey but I will find out." I handed her the phone and the new SIM and she made the call. She, actually laughed when she spoke with her friend! I hadn't heard that sound for a while! When she hung up, she fell into my arms and she said, very quietly, "We are safe, my man! We are safe, now! There are none, allowed here, in Turkey!" In the back of her mind, she was thinking about Marta, at the airport, in Madrid! We laid on the bed and held each other! Safe?

Wilf's phone rang, "Yeah?"

"Hey boss, Riley here."

Riley was their man in the National Crime Agency. "What's up, Riley?"

"Satch and some chick landed in Istanbul, a couple of hours ago."

"Istanbul huh?"

"Yep, they got in a taxi and went into the city."

"Thanks Riley, you just got a bonus." He hung up.

"Jules?"

"Yeah boss?"

"Satch's is Istanbul. Who we got there?"

"Mahoney's there with a couple of other guys. They're goin' to pick up a load of hash from that Frederick guy, in a week."

"OK, well, get him on the phone right away. I gotta talk to him."

"Sure boss." He dialed a number and handed the phone to Wilf.

"Hey Jules, what's up?"

"It's Wilf, Gary."

"Oh, hey boss, what's up?"

"A guy called Satch, just landed at Istanbul airport with some chick and I wanna know where he is."

"You got a description?"

"I'll text you his picture. Find him for me and it's worth a lot."

Mahoney laughed, "Well, OK boss, we'll find him!"

Wilf texted the photo and for 2 days there was nothing, then his phone rang. "Gary?"

"Yeah, we found him boss. He's in a little hotel on the edge of the city. He's got a nice piece with him."

"Did you see him?"

"No, but we got a good group of Turkish guys here. They know everything that's happenin' here. It's him, alright."

"OK, good, Jules and Harris'll be there in the mornin'. Have someone pick them up."

"Oh, no problem, I'll pick them up myself!"

A Trip out of Town

For two days, we wandered around Istanbul, looking at the sights and going to the many markets. We were tourists, like the thousands of others around us. I was totally surprised, when we got onto the elevator, in the hotel, when two big, black guys got on with us! One look, told me who they were;

Sutton's men! Drug dealers! I gripped Elena's hand, before the door closed and one of them, the biggest one, said, "Nope, don't even think about it, mate! We're all here, together and we're all goin' to your room!" Elena stiffened and almost fell over!

We went into the room and when the door closed, the guy said, "OK, now we got you, mate! We're gonna call Wilf and let him know." He pointed at Elena, "You, sit, there, on that chair and don't move! We got nothin' on you, so don't give us a reason, OK?" He took a gun out his pocket, pointed it and said to me, "And you sit there, on the bed!"

The other guy opened his phone and dialed a number, "Yep, Harris here; we got him boss. We're here, in Istanbul!" I could hear the laughter on the phone. "Yep, he's got a nice piece with him! Sweet little thing! Great! Yeah, thanks, we'll take a bit of it before we leave! You sendin' the plane for us? In the mornin', OK. Yeah, OK, we'll see you then!" He switched off the phone and looked at Jules, "Boss, says he's comin' here on the plane in the mornin' to that little airport on the other side of town."

"Yeah, I know where it is. We pick up hashish

there, usually."

"Yeah, that's the one." He looked at me and then he smiled at Elena, "Now, babe, me and Jules here, is gonna fuck you hard!" Elena started and Jules put his hand on her arm and shook his head when she looked at him. She relaxed; too relaxed, I thought! I moved forward,. He pointed the gun at me, "You get in that fuckin' bathroom, mate! Don't fuck about! We're gonna get some of this nice ass and there's fuck all you can do about it! Now, move!" He raised the gun and when I looked at Elena, I could see that she was smiling! What? She was going to do her job! Normal for her!

I went into the bathroom and sat on the toilet. I heard Harris say, "Get your clothes off, bitch!" In a short time, I could hear one of them moaning as he fucked her. After a short while, it stopped and then the next one was moaning. Finally, there was silence and it seemed like an hour went by. I was dying inside and I wanted to scream! I heard Jules say, "OK, suck my cock now, girl!"

I put my hands over my ears, so I wouldn't hear any more but it didn't stop the sound of the gunshot and when I took my hands away, there was second shot! I jumped to my feet and a second later, Elena pulled the door open! She was standing there, naked, with a gun in her hand! I moved forward, took the gun from her and she slumped against me. She was shaking like a leaf! "I killed those fuckers! They raped me!" she said. I took the gun from her and led her to the bed. The two black guys were covered in blood! One on the floor, the other on the bed. Elena had shot both of them in the head!

Suddenly, the door to the room flew open! The hotel owner, holding a pistol and his brother were standing there! He closed the door and the owner said, "Well, this is not good, sir!" He was smiling!

"No, it isn't," I said.

"No, it isn't," his brother, the driver said.

"It will be expensive to clean this up." The owner.

"How expensive?" I asked.

"No less than £5000, to be sure!"

"£5000, you say?" He nodded. I reached for my bag, counted out the money and said, "Good?"

He took the money, "Good!"

"Do you know how to get to Amasya?" Elena asked.

"Ah, yes, Amasya!" the driver said. "We have a good cousin there! We know it well! It is about 675 kilometers from here! Do you go to there?"

"Yes, we go," she said in Turkish! Yes, she also speaks Turkish! Traveler! She put her clothes on.

The man laughed, "Well, I will drive you there, first thing in the morning! Only £100!" He held his hand out, "Deal?"

I shook his hand, "Deal!" I peeled off the two £50 notes and the owner said, "Now, you will take a new room and we will clean up this mess, yes?" I nodded. "Good, now you go down to reception and see my daughter and she will give you the key. You should go out for dinner, somewhere and you will leave here at 7:00 in the morning for Amasya, yes?"

Things were moving too fast! We picked up our bags and went to reception. There was a teenager there. She handed the key to me, without saying anything or looking at me, like what had happened was normal in this hotel. We went to the room and Elena fell against me when I closed the door, "I had to do it!" she said, bursting into tears! I held her and pulled her to the bed. We fell onto it and she held me tighter than ever! "They raped me!" she said. "The big one hurt me! When I was sucking his cock, he put the gun down, so I picked it up and shot him in the head. The other one moved and then I shot him, too! They were raping me!" I held her and didn't speak. We laid there for over an hour and then, finally she sat up and went into the bathroom. I heard the shower running and I laid on the bed and thought about, what's next. What's next?

"Right," Billy said, "we've issued an international arrest warrant for Simon Atcheson for kidnapping and people trafficking. I've sent a copy of it to Turkey and they've responded, saying that they'll increase their efforts to find him."

George sat, looking at him, "So, what do we do now?"

"Well, the best thing, is to carry on with our investigations here. We got some excellent evidence from his flat and that dirty box he was living in and those little girls have told us about him. The Albanians aren't saying anything yet and I don't expect them to. Atcheson is traveling with a young woman. We don't know for sure but we suspect that she might be one of their sex slaves. They flew into Istanbul from Madrid and they went to Madrid from the little island of Corvo in the middle of the Atlantic. As far as we know this Atcheson has never traveled before. We've gone through passport records and he doesn't appear anywhere. The woman he's with, is called Joana Marconi. There is no record of her traveling anywhere before this, so it's probably a fake name and passport. Our boy, Satch has moved into a new realm, that's for sure."

Liz smiled, "Big steps up for a homeless guy from King's Cross!" Billy and George nodded.

George stood up, "Well, OK, let's get to it then. Not much more we can do."

A Way out

I hadn't noticed her do it, but Elena had picked up the phone that Harris had used to call Sutton. As we were going to Amasya, she handed it to me, "This is his phone." I took the phone and put it in my bag. As we got closer to Amasya, she said, "Give me your phone, now; I need to tell Ajola, we are close." She dialed the number and spoke in her language. She laughed, again! "OK, she is ready for us! She has a very big house and she says she has a nice room for us." She looked at the driver, "Do you know Polat, near the hill?"

"Yes, of course! They have a really nice house there! You go to there?" She nodded. "Good, ah well, I will take you there, no problem! They are nice family! Nice woman lives there! You know her?"

Elena nodded, "Yes, she is my friend!"

"Ah, then you are very well! The man, is big man, here in Turkey! You will be good there and please, have no fear about that rubbish at the hotel! It was taken care of! No worry there, OK?" I nodded, hoping he was right!

We arrived at a very large house with a high wall around it. "They are expecting you, no?" Elena nodded and smiled. There was a big, closed gate that had two men standing in front of it. They were wearing dark suits and one of them smiled at the driver and said, "Yes, may I help you with something?"

"We are expected," Elena said. "Elena."

He went to a phone, next the gate and spoke into it. He came back to the car and said, "Yes, the lady is waiting for you." He motioned to his mate to open the gate. We went up a long drive with mountains in the background and when we got to the house, I saw two men with small machine guns, standing in the shadows. The door opened and a very attractive, slim woman, in her mid twenties, with natural blonde hair and long legs came out. Elena squealed when she saw her! "Here is my friend!" she shouted, getting out of the car! She ran to her friend and embraced her! Both of them were crying!

I got out of the car and the driver said, "We hope, we do not see you again, my friend but if you need us, just call the hotel." He handed me a business card with the hotel telephone number on it.

A tall, dark haired man, about 50 years old came out of the house and slowly, walked down the stairs. Elena's friend pulled her to him and said, "This, Frederick, is my best friend, Elena!" Frederick held his hand out and she shook it.

"And this is my man, Satch," Elena said,

smiling. "He saved me!" They both shook my hand.

"Now, please come into the house," Frederick said. "I am sure you are tired after that long trip." We went into the tallest, longest foyer I had ever seen! There was a long, curving staircase and a crystal chandelier, shining brightly. The house was enormous! A real mansion! Frederick led us into a large parlour and motioned for us to sit on beautifully upholstered sofas. I felt like I was floating when I sat down! He held up a decanter, "Brandy?"

I nodded, Elena shook her head. Ajola said, "Come, Elena, we will make some tea and these men can drink brandy, yes?" Elena nodded and took her hand as they went out.

Frederick handed me a snifter of brandy and I took a sip. It was very nice! I said so, "Very nice, Frederick, thank you."

"You are very welcome." He sipped his brandy, "Now, what brings you here, Satch?" He was watching me closely.

"Elena and I, need to try and stop people from finding us."

"And, if they find you?"

"We will be sent to Romania, tortured and then killed to make a snuff film. On top of that, we have an English drug dealer that wants to kill me for selling his baby."

Frederick smiled, "Well, this sounds, not too good for the two of you, my friend." He sipped his brandy. "And who is this, English drug dealer?"

"A man named, Wilf Sutton."

"Ah, Wilf; I know him very well! We do business together!" I wondered what business that was. "I heard that his baby got stolen! It was you?" I nodded, cautiously. He laughed! "Well, he has his baby back! He is back with his mother. You took him to sell, didn't you?" I nodded. "And you got paid?" I nodded, again. "In this case, you should be alright. Wilf is a good man. He is a businessman, so he will not be too upset. He, only wants to make an example of you. With the right persuasion, he will stop looking for you."

"Do you know anyone that can put that kind of pressure on him?"

He laughed, "Yes, I think I do, actually! Leave it with me."

"Well, you know, I never would have taken his son, if I knew who he was. It was just business."

"That is good to know. We all make our money in our own ways. As to the Albanians, they are prohibited from coming here, to Turkey and they obey that. Our people cannot go to their country to do business, so it is all very fair. As long as you are here, you will be safe. Over time, we will work it out with them. A girl like Elena is not worth much to them, so for a small fee, you should be alright with them, too. I did the same thing with Ajola. Again, they want to set an example to their girls, that it is no use trying to escape. As you can see, though, my Ajola is here. She escaped successfully."

"How small?"

"No more than £10,000 or so. Do you have that much?" I nodded. "Good, then you will be good."

"I, also have British police looking for me, for selling babies, in the UK. I'm sure they'll start to look in Europe, soon."

His face darkened, "Ah, well, this is a bit different. I do not know how to stop them, doing their job. You are safe, here, now, though, so try and relax." He looked at my glass, "More brandy?" I nodded.

Elena and Ajola came into the room and Elena was smiling; that was very good to see! She sat next to me and put her arm around my neck, "All good with you, my man?" She looked relaxed for the first time in days!

I kissed her cheek, "Yes, all's good here. Frederick and I have been having a chat."

Ajola said, looking at Frederick, "We will have a nice meal soon. Diana is making us a big roast beef."

Frederick smiled, "Good, I want some of that."

Suddenly, we heard a mobile phone ringing. We looked around and I realised that the sound was coming from my bag. I opened it and took out the phone that Elena had picked up in the hotel room. The phone of the guy that she had shot. "Hello?"

"Who's this?"

"Who's this?"

"Where's Jules?"

"Jules?"

"Who the fuck is this?"

"This is Satch." Elena was sitting with her hand over her mouth!

"Satch! You motherfucker!"

"Who is this?"

"This is Wilf Sutton, you fucker! Where the fuck is Jules?"

"If you mean the guy that came to my room, raped my girlfriend and threatened to kidnap us and take us to meet you, then he ain't going to be talking to you, any time soon."

Silence. I waited. "Where is he?"

"He's dead."

"Dead?"

"Dead."

"What happened to him?"

"He raped my girlfriend and when she was blowing him, he put his gun on the bed and she shot him and the other guy in the head. They're both dead." I couldn't believe how calm I felt. I was talking like this was something that happened every day!

Frederick reached out for the phone. I put it into his hand. He spoke, "Wilf, Frederick."

"Frederick! What the Hell are you doin' there?"

"Well, my friend, I am in my home and Satch and Elena are my guests here."

"Your guests?"

"Yes, they came here, earlier today and now they are my guests. They told me about your friends and I have to say that I am surprised that you want bad things to happen to these good people."

"Frederick, that son of a bitch took my son and sold him!"

"And you have your son back, now, do you not?"

"Yes, after a lot of effort, I do have him back."

"So, no real damage done. I have discussed it with Satch and he has told me that if he had known it was your son, he never would have done that. So, I think it would be a good thing, if you could stop this search for him and let everyone get back to doing business. He has, after all, been found, by me."

"I need to make an example of him, Frederick."

"Yes, I'm sure that you do, my friend but violence is not the answer. How much do you think he should pay for his misdeed?"

"Let me think about it. I'll come back to you."

"Good, give me a call in a day or two. We need to discuss our next shipment."

"Yep, OK, I'll do that."

Frederick handed me the phone and smiled, "Do not worry, my friend. I do a lot of business with Wilf and I know him very well. He is a sensible and reasonable man. I'm sure it will cost you some money but all will be good, now."

Diana, the cook, a short fat woman came into the room, "Dinner is ready, sir."

We went into a dining room with a huge dining table. There was crystal and china and silverware and an excellent roast beef dinner with wine and all the trimmings! I'd never seen anything like it! As I ate, I was thinking about all those years, living in a box with the other homeless people. The conversation during dinner was lively and interesting. Elena and Ajola talked constantly, in English and in their own language, laughing and gesturing. Frederick and I, hardly spoke but we watched and laughed when they did. We were, totally relaxed!

After dinner, we went back to the parlour and Frederick and I had brandy. I felt relaxed and tired. The strain over the last couple of weeks had been intense and now that I was sitting comfortably with Elena next to me, I could hardly keep my eyes open. We went to bed and it was like I had died! I slept a dreamless sleep in a very soft bed.

The next morning, I went downstairs and found Frederick sitting on the patio, drinking a coffee. "Well, good morning Satch! I hope you slept well?"

I sat next to him. The sun was shining warmly and there were flowers everywhere, giving off their scents. I poured a coffee and sat back, listening to the birds chirping. "Yes, it was like I'd died! I was really tired and you know, what we've been through over the last weeks has been pretty intense."

"Well, just relax. Here, you are safe." I sat back and sipped the coffee. "I'm sure," he said, "you have been wondering what I do?"

I had been thinking about that since we arrived. "I have, actually."

He smiled, "Yes, well, I do business with Wilf and many people like him. I have a number of very good contacts here in Turkey and I buy and sell large quantities of hashish. It is, very lucrative business."

I nodded, "I thought that was it."

"Yes, well, it is good business."

Elena came out and sat on my lap and kissed me, "Good morning. I missed you when I woke up."

I put my arm around her, "Good morning to you. We're just sitting here, drinking coffee and having a chat."

She stood up, "Well, I'm hungry. I will go and find Ajola." She went into the house.

Frederick said, "Would you like to have some breakfast?" I nodded. "Good, let's go into the house and get Diana to make us some of her good food."

We ate a lot of food and drank more coffee and afterwards, I sat next to the swimming pool with

Elena beside me. Safety.

When Wilf Sutton put the phone down, after speaking to Satch, he wanted to scream! Frederick Holditz, the guy he had just spoken with, was one of the few people he was afraid of. Wilf had been running the drug business in the UK for almost ten years. He had respect and contacts all over the world. He'd made a fortune and he'd come a long way from the estate in Brixton that he'd grown up in. He did drug deals with a lot of people and most of them would never think of crossing him. Frederick had, initially approached him a few years ago because he needed a way into the UK drug market. He'd asked around and found out that Frederick was Swiss and well connected with most of the cartels around the world. Certainly, not someone to fuck with! Since then, they'd done an excellent business together. Now, this fucking Satch was his guest? The guy that had stolen his child? He wanted to take his frustration out on someone! "Mike!"

Mike came into the room, "Yes, boss?"

"Call the pilot and tell him to get the jet ready! I'm goin' to Turkey!"

"Yes, OK boss. When do you want to leave?"

"Right away!"

"OK boss."

A Proposition

Frederick came outside, dressed in a blue shirt and a pair of khaki shorts. He sat next to me in a lounger and smiled, "So, Satch, what will you and Elena do now?"

I looked at him. He was very fit and had a good tan. "I'm not sure, yet, Frederick. I know we have to do something. Elena tells me, the Albanians have a very long reach and she says that there's nowhere we can go to escape them."

"Well, as I told you yesterday, it is possible to pay a sum of money and then they will leave you alone."

"Do you know how to contact them?"

He smiled, "Yes, of course I do. I had to do the same for Ajola. She was in Miami at the time. Like me, they are also business people."

I nodded, "Good, could you contact them for me?"

"You took her from Portugal, yes?"

"Yes, she was in a house in a little place called Penafiel, in the north."

"Well, it will be up to the person you took her from to accept the payment. I will contact the people I know and see what can be arranged. It will take a few days."

I smiled, "Well, we're very comfortable here, so please, see if you can make contact with them."

"Yes, I will do that today." He went into the house.

Two hours went by and he called me. I went into the house and he motioned for me to sit in a chair in front of a large walnut desk. "I have spoken with a man, I know in Albania. He will contact their Portuguese man and let me know in a few days, what is going to happen. He was sure that it is possible to pay something for her and be done with this."

"That's great! Whatever it costs, I'll pay it! We just want to be done with this!"

"Have you much money, Satch?"

"Yes, I have something, under £80,000."

He frowned, "Not a lot. Would you like to make an investment?"

"An investment?"

"Yes.

"What kind of investment?"

"Well, I deal in large quantities of hashish which I sell around the world. For example, Wilf is coming here soon to buy 200 kilos. His friends will come with him and they will take the hashish to the

UK in his private jet. We have been doing this business for a few years and it has been very profitable for us."

"And you want me to invest in hashish?"

"Yes, if you would like to. You could give me, let's say, £50,000, and in a week, I will double or triple that. No risk to you."

"Would I need to handle the drugs?"

He laughed, "No, certainly not! I do not handle the drugs and I make millions! I have people for that."

£50,000! "I'd like to think about it for a bit."

"Of course, there is no hurry. You are welcome to stay here with Elena for as long as you want to. You are my guests and Ajola loves having her here. I got a call from Wilf Sutton, this morning. He will be here this afternoon with his men. We have business to do and he says that he wants to meet with you, to discuss recompense."

I was sweating now. "OK, I guess so. Do I have a choice?"

He laughed, again, "No, I am afraid you do not. He will want something from you, so it is best if you do the business with him and be done with this."

I stood up, "Well, OK, let me know when he gets here." I went back out to the pool to sit next to Elena.

"So, what now Satch? Elena asked. She was wearing a very small, red bikini and she looked delicious with her dark tan!

"Now, we are waiting to see how much money, Sr. Anibal wants for your freedom. When the money is paid, we will be free of the Albanians for good."

She laughed, "Is it, really that simple?"

I took her hand, "Apparently, yes. Frederick told me that he paid for Ajola and now they have no more problems."

"But what about the drug dealers?"

"Wilf Sutton is coming here with his men, today, to pick up a load of hashish and he wants to meet with me. He'll want money too."

"Have you enough money to pay for all of this?"

"I hope so. Frederick asked me if I want to invest in a drug deal."

"And will you do that?"

"If I have any money left over, after all of this, probably I will."

"Will we have to transport the drugs?" She was looking worried now.

"No, just invest the money and take the profit."

She shook her head, "I hope we will be alright."

Wilf Sutton was looking out the window of the jet. He said, "OK Matt, when we touch down, I want you and Miles to get a truck and go to the warehouse. Wait there for my call. We're pickin' up 200 kilos. I'll go to see my guy and finish the deal."

"OK boss, will do."

The jet landed and Wilf got into a waiting car. Five hours later, he got to Frederick's house. He'd been there before and it was one of the few places that he felt like someone else was in control. He was eager to meet with Frederick, again and he wanted to look Satch in the eye! The men on the gate opened it, without looking at him and when he got to the house, Frederick came out to meet him, "Welcome, my friend! Good to see you, again!"

Wilf shook his hand, "It's good to be here, Frederick."

They walked into the house, "And how was your journey up here?"

"Nice, very nice. I got a new jet. It's bigger than the other one, so traveling on it is very nice."

"Well, very good. Come in and have a brandy." They sat on sofas and Wilf looked around the room. He was, always impressed when he came to this place. He liked the paintings and the sculptures and he could see how successful Frederick was. He wanted all of it! Frederick smiled at him, "Are your people standing by?"

"Yes, they should be at the warehouse now."

"Good, I will have the goods released."

"Where is Satch?"

"Satch is here. Would you like to speak with him?"

Wilf was seething! "Yes, I would," he said,

through gritted teeth!

Frederick went out of the room, called me and we went into the parlour. "Sit here, Satch."

I'd never been so nervous! I'd never met Wilf but I knew all about him! All of the homeless people knew of him. Wilf looked at me, sipped his brandy and said, "Usually, you'd be dead by now." I didn't know what to say, so I said nothing. "What do you have to say for yourself?"

I could see that he wanted to hit me! "I'm sorry, Wilf. If I'd known it was your baby, I never would've taken him. I got an order for a small, black, baby boy, so I did what they asked. It could've been any kid."

"But it wasn't any kid; it was mine!" he shouted. "Do you have any idea how my wife reacted when she heard about it? And what kind of a fuckin' business, is stealin' babies, anyway!" I squirmed but didn't speak. I was terrified! Frederick looked on, smiling.

"What do you want, Wilf?" I asked.

Wilf finished his brandy, "How much did they pay you?"

I lied. "They paid me, £15,000."

"£15,000 for my child?" I nodded. "£15,000!" He looked at Frederick, "I'm sure they get a lot more for them on the market, don't they."

Frederick laughed, "The amounts of money in that business are enormous! I have considered it myself but I cannot imagine doing it. It is most unsavoury to me, selling babies and parts of babies, putting them in those dirty films!"

"Yeah, I'm with you there!" He looked at me. "Right, I want the £15,000 and" he reached into his pocket and took out a long flick knife, "I'll take one of your fingers."

He said it, so casually that, at first I couldn't understand what he'd said. I opened my fingers and said, "One of my fingers?"

He flicked the knife open, "Yes, and feel lucky that I'm not takin' your whole fuckin' hand!"

I wanted to run! I looked at Frederick. He was watching me, closely. "Which finger?"

"I'll let you decide that."

Fuck! Which finger? He stood up and went over to a part of the room, with no carpets. "Come over here." I stood up. I was trembling. "Come on! Get the fuck over here!" I walked over to him. "Hold out your left hand." I held my hand out. "Which finger?" I opened my fingers and he grabbed the small one and in one smooth motion he cut it off and stood there holding it! I expected pain but didn't feel any! I looked at my hand and saw the blood running out of it and dripping onto the floor! The finger was gone; just a small stump was left. He threw it onto the floor!

Frederick stood up and calmly said, "Go into the kitchen, Satch. Diana will fix that up for you."

I was in shock! I went into the kitchen and saw Diana standing beside the big table. When she saw my hand, she moved forward and said something to me that I couldn't understand. She motioned to a chair and I sat on it. I felt like fainting! She got a first aid box and took out some bandages. She was talking to me but I couldn't understand her. My hand was beginning to hurt. Elena came in with Ajola. They were dressed in bikinis and smiling. When Elena saw my hand, she shrieked, "Oh my God, Satch, what has happened to you?" She grabbed my hand and I winced in pain! She put her arms around me and wept.

"Wilf Sutton took his payment!"

When Diana finished bandaging my hand, I went back to the parlour. Frederick stood up and went to the drinks table. He held up a decanter, "Brandy, Satch?" No, how are you?

I sat on a sofa, "Yes, please, Frederick." My hand was throbbing!

Wilf looked at me, "Just business, Satch." I saw that my finger was still on the floor in a pool of blood!

Frederick handed me the brandy, "So, now our business is done, yes? No hard feelings, now?"

I took a long drink of the brandy and handed him the empty snifter and looked at Wilf, "We're, even now?"

Wilf held up his glass, "You pay me the 15 grand and we're even!"

Frederick handed me the refilled glass; I held it up, "Good." My hand hurt!

Frederick sat down and smiled, "I got a call from Portugal, Satch; Sr. Anibal. He wants you to pay

20,000 Euros for Elena. Then, you will both be free!"

"20,000!" He nodded. Fuck, after I paid that and Wilf, that would leave me with less than £50,000! "OK, if that's what he wants, I'll pay it."

Wilf nodded, "You're movin' up, kid."

I finished my brandy and went up to my room and laid on the bed. My hand on fire!

Billy Bridges called his task force together, "We've had word that, Simon Atcheson is at the home of one of the biggest dealers in cannabis resin in Europe."

George laughed, "What the Hell is he doing there?" A few others laughed too! "He's a friggin' homeless guy!"

Liz said, "What the Hell is he doing?"

"Here's the best part," Billy said. "Wilf Sutton is with him!"

George looked at Liz, "Have we missed something on this guy? Everything we know, says that he's just a harmless, homeless guy and now he's with big time drug dealers? What the Hell is happening here?"

Billy shook his head, "I don't know, George but, look; I'm disbanding this task force from today. We've gathered a huge amount of evidence on this guy and we've done all we can, as a team on this. We've got some of the principles in the people trafficking part of it, locked up and we know where Satch is. Everyone can go back to their usual jobs and I want to thank all of you for your hard work on this. George and you, Liz will continue to work on it, as it's still your case and hopefully, soon, the Turkish police will help us out." Everyone stood up and started talking to each other.

George and Liz went to sit at their desks, "What the fuck is happening here, Liz? I mean, who is this guy, Satch?"

Liz smiled and picked up a sheet of paper, "He's a shoplifter with a juvenile record. That's it!"

George sipped his tea, "Well, now, he's a people trafficker, stealing and selling babies and he's tied to the biggest drug dealer in the UK and one of the biggest drug dealers in the world! Where does that leave us?" She put the sheet of paper down and shrugged.

Chief Inspector Idris Aksoy of the Directorate General of the Turkish National Police got the international arrest warrant for Satch. There was a photo and a report attached. He'd been a police officer for over 20 years. He sat at his desk, looking at it and smiled. 'A people trafficker, baby stealer. English! Ah, these English'! he thought as he looked at it. He picked up the phone and called his partner, "Come to me, Atlan."

Atlan, a tall, thin, balding man came into the room and sat in front of his desk. "What's up, partner?" Idris handed him the arrest warrant. He read it and smiled, "Another, bastard Englishman! Why do these people come here to our country?"

"I do not know, Atlan but we must find out where he is. I have a report here, that he is travelling with a woman and that he went to a hotel in Istanbul. From there, we don't know but we will go to that hotel and we will find out. Let's go, now!"

They went to the hotel that Satch had stayed at and they found the owner. Idris showed him the photo, "This man stayed here? The owner nodded. He knew better, than to lie to the Turkish police and, of course, Satch meant nothing to him. Turkish prisons are not nice places and they do torture people! "Where did he go when he left here?"

The owner looked at the photo and smiled, "He went to the home of Frederick Holditz in Amasya."

Idris looked at Atlan, "Amasya?" The hotel owner smiled and nodded. Idris turned to go, "Let's go, Atlan." The hotel owner smiled as they went out. He knew that they wouldn't be bothering him any more. Frederick was one of the protected ones in Turkey.

They went back to their office. When they arrived, Idris sat, heavily in his chair. "I will send a report." He knew there was nothing he could do. Frederick was very well connected in Turkey!

Payday

Elena came into the room and sat beside me, "Oh, Satch! How is your hand?" Tears were running down her cheeks.

I held up my hand, "It's painful; it's throbbing

and I'm missing a finger!"

"Is it because of me?" She carefully took my hand.

I smiled, "No, it had nothing to do with you, my love. This was about Wilf's baby. I need to pay Sr. Anibal, 20,000 Euros for you and then we're free!"

She laughed loudly! "That's it?" She squeezed my hand and I winced in pain! I nodded. "If your hand did not hurt so much, I would give you a good blow job, right now!"

I took my hand away and said, "That's just what I need, right now! Go ahead!" She did and it was very good!

Later, I went down to the parlour and found Wilf and Frederick, still drinking brandy, "So, here you are, Satch!" He looked at my hand, "Everything OK?" I nodded, as he handed me a brandy. "Good! We have been discussing business. I told Wilf, that you are interested in investing in a deal with me."

I sat on the sofa next to him, "Well, I would like to do that, but I'm not sure I have enough cash left over, what with paying Wilf and Sr. Anibal, as well. I think, I'll, only, have around £40,000 left."

"Well, that is sufficient, to get you started. If you give that to me, then I'm sure that we can improve on that, quite a bit in a short time." He looked at Wilf, "What, think you, Wilf?"

Wilf smiled, "That's a lot more than I had when I got started."

I nodded, "OK, then, let's do it!"

Ajola came into the room, "Dinner is ready Frederick. A nice meal!"

After dinner, I went to my room and counted out £15,000 to give to Wilf. The bag had been full of money and now it was almost empty! I went downstairs and handed the cash to Wilf, "Here it is, Wilf."

He took the cash from me and said, "Alright, Satch, our business is done. I'll let my people know, then you won't hear from us again." He looked at my hand, "Maybe the next time you think of takin' a baby from someone, you'll think better of it." I nodded, feeling my hand throbbing. He looked at Frederick, "As usual, it's been good doin' business with you, Frederick. I'll be in touch."

"Yes, my friend," he said, "your shipment is at the airport waiting for you." Wilf smiled at me, nodded at Frederick and went out. "You got away very lightly, my friend," Frederick said to me. "I have known Wilf to kill someone and their whole family, for nothing more than speaking to him, in a way that he did not like. You stole his child! Very lightly, indeed!"

"Well, I'm sure you had something to do with that, Frederick and I thank you for it."

"So, now to the Albanians. I have paid them the 20,000 Euros, so you can pay me for that and if you want to get involved in some business, give me what you can afford and it will be a very good investment for you and Elena."

"Yes, OK, I'll do that now." I went to my room and took out what was left of my money. 20,000 Euros was over £15,000 and then I counted out another £45,000 for the investment. I was down to £5,000! Almost nothing! I took the money downstairs and handed it to him.

He took the cash, put it into his desk drawer, without counting it and said. "Good, now my young friend, I think it is a good idea for you to take a break and relax for a while. By the end of the week, I will have doubled your investment or more, so why don't you take your girl out to the pool and relax. The weather is very good and here you are, finally safe, yes?"

"Yes, thank you, Frederick, I'll do that."

"We know where the son of a bitch is, so why can't we get him back here?" George was very upset! The task force was broken up and he and Liz were sitting at their desks. George had a report from the Turkish police and reading between the lines, he knew that it was bullshit! "After all the work we've done on this and these people are saying that they have no access to him! This, Frederick Holditz guy is one of the major drug dealers in Europe, so I'm sure he's paying off, big money to someone in their police department!"

Liz sipped her tea, "Well, there's nothing we can do from here, George, now, is there."

George stood up, holding the report in his fist, "Well, fuck it, I'm going to speak with Billy!" He strode off! Liz watched him go, smiled and shrugged.

"Billy, I need to speak with you."

Billy sat back in his chair, "Sure, what's up, mate?" He knew what was coming.

George held out the report, "This says, that the Turkish police know where Satch is and they can't go and get him! What's happening here?"

Billy looked at the copy of the report he had on his desk, "Yes, that's what it is says, doesn't it."

George sat down in a chair, heavily, "So, what're we gonna do about it?"

Billy smiled at him, "Do, George?"

George sat forward, "Yes, do! We've got this guy in a major drug dealer's house in Turkey! He's behind a big wall and the Turks say they can't touch him! So, what are we gonna do about it?"

Billy picked up the report, "This, Chief Inspector Idris Aksoy, says that it's complicated and they're working on it."

"Working on it?"

"That's what he says."

"Why don't Liz and I go to Turkey and see if we can help him out?"

Billy laughed, "Oh, great idea, George! A nice little trip for you and your partner, to Turkey, eh? Do you think we have the budget for that? This guy is a baby stealer, not a major criminal!"

"So, what do we do; just sit here and wait for him to come home? We might be waiting, for a long time for that!"

"OK, let me think on it, for a while George. In the meantime, you carry on, tying up any loose ends, so that when we finally do lay hands on him, we'll be ready."

George shook his head and stood up. When he got back to his desk, he looked at Liz, "Fuck all!"

Time to Leave

At the end of the week, after dinner, one evening, I was speaking with Frederick in the parlour. We were drinking brandy, as usual. He went to his desk, took out a large envelope and handed it to me. "This is the return on your investment, my friend."

I opened the envelope and there was £100,000 in it! I felt my eyes pop out of my head! "Wow, that's amazing! How much is here?"

"£100,000, and there can be more if you want to re-invest it with me."

I handed the envelope to him, "Yes, please!"

He laughed, "Yes, I thought you would say that! Believe me when I say, that, to see my girl Ajola so happy, it is worth much more than that to me! It will be doubled again, or more by the end of next week!" He put the envelope back in his desk. "We will continue until you are ready to leave this place."

"Leave?"

"Well, of course, I know that you will not stay here forever, although you are welcome to stay as long as you wish. Ajola is like a very happy, little girl, now that she has Elena here but we know that one day you will leave. Have you any idea where you might go?"

I hadn't even thought of it. "Well, no, I

haven't given it any thought."

"Well, I have some good friends in Brazil and some places in Central America, that you might want to consider. It is warm and inexpensive in that part of the world and I know that you would be safe. Of course, now you are free of the Albanians, so Europe is open to you. There are some very nice places in the Far East, also, like Vietnam, Thailand and Cambodia that will welcome you and your money. The English police may find you in Europe but the other places are too far away for them. For sure, you can never go back to the UK and I'm sure that Elena does not want to go back to her home. In a few weeks time, you will be a millionaire and you can then, go anywhere you wish to go. Give it some thought and in the meantime, relax some more."

"OK, I'll do that." I finished my brandy and went out to the pool. Elena was sitting with Ajola, "Well, ladies, how goes it?"

Elena patted the seat beside her, "Sit here, Satch. Ajola and I have been discussing our next move."

"Have you? I've been speaking with Frederick

about it, too. Do you know where you want to go?"

She smiled and took my injured hand and stroked it, "Well, Frederick has a nice, little island in the Caribbean with a house that is empty. Maybe we should go there."

My hand hurt but I let her hold it, "That sounds very nice."

She kissed my hand and looked at Ajola and smiled, "Yes, I think it does. Should we go there?"

"I don't see why not."

"Frederick has a jet," Ajola said, "and I'm sure he would let you use it to get there. Normal airlines are not safe for you because of the British police."

I nodded and looked at Elena, "OK, so when do you want to go?"

Ajola laughed, "You see, Elena, that was easy wasn't it!"

Elena laughed too, "Yes, it was!"

Wilf Sutton sat in his jet on the trip back to London. He was more angry than he had been on the trip into Turkey! He'd let Satch off, as easily as he had because of his business relationship with Frederick! He was his own man and had made his way up, the hard way. He'd grown up in a filthy estate in Brixton and had had to fight for everything he had! Now, he ran the county line drug network in the UK and had more than 1000 people, mostly young teenagers working for him in houses all over the country. They sold and distributed all kinds of illegal drugs, including heroin, cocaine and cannabis and they had a lot of grow houses full of illegal immigrants, growing marijuana. The profits were huge! Frederick was just one of his suppliers but he needed him to do business and he was not a guy, to upset! He was all about keeping his little whore happy and Wilf had had to go along with him!

He didn't know the people traffickers very well. He'd always steered clear of that business. He knew the Albanians were in London and other UK cities and he intended to contact them when he got back. He wanted them to do something, about this fucking Satch!

When he got back to London, he made sure

that the hashish was unloaded and sent to his people and then, when he was in his limo, he got on the phone and called a woman he knew in the prostitution business in Soho, in London. "Genevieve, it's Wilf."

"Ah Wilf, my darlin'! How are you?"

"Yes, I'm very good, love."

"Do you want, another young one?"

"No, I have some business to discuss with you."

"Business, you say? Well, I'm here! Come on over!"

"I'll be there, right away."

Wilf told his driver, where to go and when they got to Genevieve's place, he went inside. She held her arms out to him, "Come here, love, give Jenny a big kiss!"

Wilf embraced her and kissed her, "Good to see you, love."

Jenny pointed at her girls, "Maddy, is right there, Wilf. I know how much she likes you!"

Wilf looked at Maddy, a young, very attractive red head, about 19 years old. She had small breasts, long legs and bright blue eyes. Wilf always had a very good time with her She knew, exactly what to do to turn him on! "Maybe later; I need to speak with you about something important."

She took his hand, "Well, then, come into my parlour." They went into a small office and she closed the door and sat on a red, leather love seat and patted the place next to her. "What's up?"

He sat next to her, "Do you know, any Albanians?"

She was surprised, "Albanians?"

"Yes, I need to make contact with them."

"Fuck, you're not going into that business are you?" She knew that Wilf was all about the drugs!

He laughed, "No, but I need their help."

She shook her head, "They're dangerous bastards, Wilf! You need to be very careful with them! It's a nasty business they're in, what with stealin' babies and kids to put in their dirty films! I've met a few of their slaves and those girls are ruined! I've tried a few of them here but they're broken! What do you want with them, anyway?"

"You know my boy got stolen, right?"

"Yes, and I heard you got him back! That was a lucky one!"

"Yes, I did and when I was in Turkey, I met with the guy that took him. I was forced to buy him off and I'm not satisfied. I know that he was workin' for the Albanians and that he paid them off, but I want somethin' more!"

She shook her head, "OK, well, I know someone that knows someone, so leave it with me. I'll be in touch when I knows more." She stood up, "Now, how about a little romp with your favourite girl, then, eh?"

Wilf stood up. He was already erect, "Yeah, that sounds good!"

Jenny stroked his cock and said, "Maddy, Wilf wants you!"

The next morning, Wilf was in his house when the phone rang, "Yeah, who is it?"

"It's me." Jenny.

"What's up love?"

"I'm going to text you a number. You never got it from me, OK?"

"OK, love, no worries." The text message

arrived and Wilf called the number."

Flutura Toska answered the call, "Yes."

"This is Wilf Sutton."

"Yes, what do you want Mr. Sutton?" She knew who he was and she felt the same, about black people, as all of her colleagues did! Disgust!

"I need to meet you, to discuss some business."

"We have no business in common."

"We do, actually. Satch!"

"When?"

"Today?"

"3:00 at my restaurant." She switched off the phone.

At 3:00, Wilf arrived at Flutura's restaurant in north London. He was met at the door by a very large body guard. He was searched and let in. Except for Flutura and Guzim, the restaurant was empty. He sat at a booth with them and a waiter brought coffee. Flutura waved him away and looked at Wilf, "Now, what do you want?" She didn't like him and she wasn't afraid to show it!

"Satch."

Guzim shifted in his eat. "He paid."

Wilf looked at him, "Paid, is not good enough! He took my son! I want him dead!"

Flutura wanted to yawn, "You got your son back; you hurt some of our people in the process and Satch has paid our man in Portugal for his bitch. What, do you want more?"

Wilf had a briefcase with him. He put it on the table and opened it. "£25,000; I want him, taken care of."

Flutura looked at the money and closed the briefcase. "You know where he is, now, don't you?"

"Yes, I do."

"We may not do this kind of business in Turkey. You know that. As long as he is there, there is nothing we can do. It is better for you to make your own arrangements." She patted the briefcase, "And this would not be enough." She sat back in the booth and took a sip of her coffee. Business was done. Wilf stood up, picked up the briefcase and walked out, without saying anything. He got into his limo and told the driver to take him home.

The Blue Sea

For six weeks, I laid by the pool with Elena and Ajola and every week, Frederick came to me with a smile and more and more money. I kept re-investing it and I, now had over £3 million! I was rich! My hand was healed and, although I was missing a finger, I hardly noticed it, anymore. One afternoon, after lunch, Elena said, "Time for us to go, Satch!"

"Go?"

She laughed, "Yes, go! That island is waiting for us! We must go there!"

We were laying on a big, double lounger. The sun was shining; I was drinking a rum and coke and I felt very good! Our problems were behind us! "Why, now?"

"Because, we have been here long enough. It is time for us to move on. We can go to Frederick's island and decide where we will go after that. It will be nice!"

I rolled onto my side and put my arm around her, "Do we have to?"

She, lightly slapped my face, "Yes, Mr. Lazy, we have to! In the morning. Ajola will come with us. It will be good."

"Ajola will come with us?

"Yes, she will. It will be fun for us!"

I went to see Frederick, "So, you are off, my

friend," he said, smiling.

"Yes, it looks like it." I smiled, "I've been given my orders!"

He laughed, "Well, good; my girl will go with you and I know that it will be very good for you. I have a new Gulfstream, which we very much enjoy. She has a range of 7500 miles, so you will get there without having to refuel. The island is called Little Whale Cay. It has a runway, so the pilot will take you directly there. It is a short trip of a few hours and you will be taken care of, along the way. I'm sorry, I cannot join you but I must stay here to do business. Will I continue to invest your money for you?"

"Yes please."

He handed me a small booklet, "I have opened an account for you in the Caymans. It currently holds 2 million pounds. I will invest the rest in some new deals and there will be more as we go along. You will soon be very rich! I hope we can continue to do business together."

I took the booklet and laughed! "Yes, of course we will!"

The next morning, we got into a limo that

took us to a small airport, close by. I'd said goodbye to Frederick and he assured me that he would continue to invest my money in his hashish deals. The jet sat, gleaming on the runway. Inside, it was like Frederick's house! Plush sofas and gleaming wood. A very nice looking, smiling woman brought me a rum and coke and wine for the ladies! When we were airborne, I sat back, on a very soft sofa with Elena by my side and I looked out the window and smiled. This is how the rich live and now I was one of them!

Wilf's mobile rang. He looked at it; Turkey! "Yeah?"

"Satch's is on the move, boss."

Wilf sat up, "Where's he goin'?" He'd been waiting for this call!

"Frederick's private jet, so don't know yet."

"Well, find out! I want that fucker!"

"Will do, boss." Wilf put the phone down and smiled.

Flutura got a similar call. She had told her people in Turkey, who were not supposed to be there, to watch Satch and now, here was the call. "Good, well find out. We want Elena in a film! We have a client that is going to pay a lot to see her suffer!"

George Mason was sitting at his desk when the call came in. He was not used to sitting, doing nothing! Billy had never followed up on his request for him and Liz to go to Turkey and he was fed up with the constant spinning in circles, getting nowhere! "A private jet, you say?"

"Yes, sir. They left this morning in a private jet. Satch and two women. One of them is his girlfriend and the other is the girlfriend of Frederick Holditz."

"So, where are they going?"

"We haven't seen the flight manifest yet, so we don't know. The Turks are very reluctant to let out information on their rich citizens."

"Well, this fuckin' Frederick guy is Swiss for fuck sake!"

"Yes, that may be so, but he's rich, so protected here. We'll find out and let you know where they've gone."

"OK, do that and let me know as soon as you find out." He went to see Billy.

Thirteen hours and over 6000 miles, after taking off, we landed at Frederick's island, Little Whale Cay. We'd been flying over the ocean and I watched it change colour from a dark green to a nice, easy on the eyes, blue. There were a lot of small islands and when we touched down, I could see a huge, gleaming white mansion with a very nice, white sand beach!

Last Chapter

"They've gone to Frederick's island in the Caribbean. It's called Little Whale Cay."

Wilf laughed, "Thanks Charlie; bonus for you!"

"Thanks boss!"

Wilf called his man in Kingston, Jamaica, "Willy, Wilf!"

"Hey man, it's about time you called me! When you comin' here?"

"I'll be there, tomorrow."

"Alright! That's a pleasant surprise! I'll make sure, little Dina is here! Let us know the time and the boys'll pick you up!" Wilf rang off.

""They are on a small island, in the Caribbean, owned by Frederick Holditz."

Flutura smiled, "Do you know which island that is?"

"We will know that before the day is out."

"Good, thank you." She put the phone down and called Guzim.

"Yes, Flutura?"

"They are in the Carib. I will know, exactly where, very soon. We will alert Esad in Miami and get them to pick up Elena."

"Yes, Flutura." She smiled and sipped her coffee. She wanted to be there when they made the film! She would enjoy, seeing Elena squirm and scream! She might even participate in the torture, just for the fun of it! The idea excited her because she'd done it in the past, to other girls!

George had filed his last report just as his phone rang, "Yes?"

"Donovan, here, sir."

"What have you got, Donovan?"

"They boarded a private jet, bound for an island, owned by Frederick Holditz; Little Whale Cay. Should be landing there, soon."

'Thank fuck for that'! George thought. "OK, son, thank you. Send me the details."

He went to see Billy. "Satch and his girl went to the Caribbean, today, on a private jet."

Billy sat up and smiled, "Where in the Caribbean, do you know?"

"A private island called Little Whale Cay,

owned by Holditz."

He laughed, "I guess, you want, you and Liz to take a trip there, to pick him up?"

George leaned against the door frame and smiled, "Now, that's an excellent idea! I could use some sunshine! I hear the rum is good, too!"

"I'll see what we can do."

George saluted and went back to his desk. Liz saw him smiling, "What's made you so happy?"

"Do you fancy going to the Caribbean for a few days?"

She laughed, "Sure, I'll get my sun screen! I'll bring my bikini too, shall I?"

"Good, you might need it! Satch and his girl went there on a private jet this morning. Billy said that he might, get us to go there and pick him up."

She sipped her tea, "I'll believe that when I see it!"

Frederick's place in Turkey had been luxurious but the mansion we were now in, was right out of a Hollywood movie! On two floors with a large swimming pool, a Jacuzzi, private beach, a butler, three house maids, a gardener, a cook and rooms that were on the edge of the sea! Total privacy!

Elena pulled me onto the bed when we got into the bedroom and took her clothes off. She pulled off my pants and straddled me. We made love passionately! When we were finished and lying side by side, she said, "That is just the start, Satch! Tonight, you will have, both me and Ajola!"

"What?"

She laughed, "Ajola has wanted you for a long time, now. She could do nothing while we were with Frederick but now, she wants to do a threesome with us. We did many of them when we were working together and we have made love, together, many times in Turkey."

I sat up, "You and Ajola made love?"

She held my cock which was stiffening, "Yes, many times." She took my cock in her mouth and moaned.

"Little Whale Cay, boss."

"Good, thanks." Wilf was in Kingston, "Do you know, Little Whale Cay, Willy?"

"Private island, right?"

"Yeah, owned by Frederick Holditz, a Swiss guy, I know."

"We'll find it. Harbert!"

"Yes, boss."

"Little Whale Cay! Find out where it is!"

"Yes, boss!"

"Dina, treat you alright, Wilf?"

"As she always does, Willy; as she always does!"

"Little Whale Cay."

Flutura smiled, "Good, thank you. Guzim!"

"Yes, Flutura?"

"Call Adesa! Little Whale Cay."

"Yes, Flutura."

George went to see Billy. He was on the internet. "Little Whale Cay is 817 clicks from Jamaica, 246 from Miami and only 21 from Nassau. Little place. Looks like it has its own runway."

George looked at the monitor. "Well, I guess we fly to Nassau and it's a short boat ride from there."

Billy laughed, "I'll have to pull a few strings, first! Need to contact the Bahamian police to let them know what we need. You sure you want to go?"

George laughed, "The sooner the better! Let's, go get the little bastard!"

We settled down on the beach and sat, drinking rum and coke in the warm sunshine. Hot sun, small waves, two beautiful, naked woman lying next to me and I felt like I was in paradise! As I lay there, I thought about the box, I had been sleeping in, next to King's Cross Station in London with Kylie and all of the other homeless people as my neighbours. Such a short time and my life had been turned, completely around! I was rich and didn't really understand what that meant! I looked at the large, well furnished mansion behind me and smiled. 'It looks like this, I guess'!

"You feel good, baby?" Elena touched my hand where Wilf had cut off my finger.

"Yes, I feel really good!"

Ajola rolled onto her side and propped her head up on her hand, "You gonna fuck us tonight, Satch?" She moved her hand over her shaved vulva and licked her lips.

My cock started to harden, "Why wait, until tonight?"

She smiled, rolled onto her back and opened her legs, "OK, let me see what you've got." I stood up, my cock standing tall and got between her legs. She guided my cock into her, looked at Elena and said something in their language; Elena nodded and smiled. I slid my cock into her and moaned. She was very tight! Elena was next and afterwards we went into the house and showered together.

"OK Wilf, we gots the boat ready. It's gonna take us a few hours to get there, so we got the beer loaded up and we're ready to go!"

"OK, let's get to it! Got the weapons?"

"Got 'em!"

"Let's go, then!" It was a long, red cigarette boat with a top speed of fifty knots. It was, usually used to run large quantities of drugs into the US, through Key West. "This is the boat we used to run coke from, from Brazil, ain't it?" Wilf said, smiling.

"The very one, mate! I thought you'd recognise her! Get ready for a rough ride!" The engine roared and they bounced over the waves!

"We'll take the yacht," Adesa said. "It's Flutura, in London that wants this girl, so we have to be sure we do it right. She has a direct contact to our people in Albania, so it's got to be right! No messing up! We get about 30 knots out of the yacht, so we'll leave, early in the morning. We pick up the girl and get right back here! Let's go!"

"George, Liz, come in here please." George winked at Liz and they went into Billy's office. "Sit, you two. I've gotten permission for the two of you to go and pick up this Satch guy in the Bahamas. The police, there, will wait for you and pick you up at the airport in Nassau. They say, that they know of this Little Whale Cay. It's usually rented out to tourists but it's owned by Fredrick Holditz and his people are always there. They say that they don't expect any trouble when you're there."

"When do we go?" George asked.

"Go home, pack a small bag, each and your flight leaves in three hours. We'll have a car drop you at Heathrow." He looked at George, "This isn't a holiday, George; it's work! You'll be there, for no more than three days."

"Time for a couple of rum and cokes though, I hope." Billy smiled and made a shooing motion and George and Liz went out and high fived each other. They went home and packed a small bag, each. Liz packed her sun screen and her bikini!

We went to bed early. I'd never been involved in a threesome or seen two women have sex together but that night I had an education. They were experts and very used to doing things to each other in bed. In between my orgasms, they made love to each other and had countless orgasms! It was a very good time! First time for everything!

The next afternoon, we were eating lunch on the terrace, next to the pool, when a long, very good looking, dark red, motor boat came into the little harbour. The engine was growling. There were five black men onboard and as I ate some bread, I watched them tie up the boat and step out of it, onto the dock. One of them looked familiar! Wilf Sutton!

Fuck! I grabbed Elena's arm, "Wilf Sutton is here, babe!"

Elena looked at me, shocked, looked at the guys getting out of the boat, and said something to Ajola. They both jumped up and ran into the house, Ajola shouting something in their language! "Come, this way!" Ajola said, running! The butler and one of the house servants, appeared with small machine guns! We went up the stairs and Ajola said, "There is a safe room, next to my bedroom! We will go in there and lock the door!" We followed her into a small room with a very thick door. "We are safe here." She closed the door. "They cannot open this room without a lot of explosives. Frederick, had it built for this reason!"

There were four monitors in the room, that showed the CCTV around the estate. We saw Wilf and his four guys approach the house. They were armed and they stopped when they saw our two guys, now three guys with weapons. "Stop there!" the butler said. "What do you want here?"

Wilf, stepped forward, "We're here for Satch! We're takin' him with us!"

The butler shook his head, "There is no one here by that name! You have the wrong house!"

We could see on the monitor, that another boat, a large, white yacht came into the harbour. Six men got out of it. Ajola, said something to Elena in their language and she slumped to the floor. "That is Ajola's, old boss man from Miami," Elena said. "The one that she escaped from! He is here to take us with him!"

As the six, approached the house, they could see Wilf and his men and the butler with our guys. They took out some weapons and walked, slowly, cautiously, towards the house. When they arrived on the patio, the one in the lead, looked at Wilf and said, smiling, "Is this a meeting?" He looked very confident. It looked like a small army of men, now!

Wilf stepped back and smiled, also and held out his hand, "I'm Wilf Sutton. I'm here to pick up a friend of ours."

Adesa shook his hand, "We, too are here to pick up a friend. A young lady."

"I guess that'll be, our friend's girlfriend?"

"Perhaps, yes, it may be. We are to bring her

to our friends in Romania. She will be in a film, there."

"Well, I guess, all we have to do, is get past these guys and we'll be able to do our business." He lifted his weapon a bit higher. I could see how nervous the butler was. He was, very outgunned by the visitors!

As we watched the monitors, we saw a large boat with the words Coast Guard on its side and the Bahamian flag at its masthead. Six, armed, uniformed men got out of it, followed by a man and woman, dressed in normal summer clothes; shorts and T shirts. They walked towards the house and when the others saw them, they started to move away from the house. When the lead officer got to the house, he showed his badge and said, "We are here for Simon Atcheson."

The butler lowered his weapon, "He is upstairs with our mistress, sir."

"Lead me to him."

The butler brought them upstairs and the officer knocked on the door. "Simon Atcheson; open the door, now, please."

I looked at Elena, kissed her and opened the door. "Well, we meet at last, Satch," the guy in the shorts and T shirt said.

The End

Epilogue

That was almost six years ago. Now, I'm sitting here, almost thirty years old, in my box next to King's Cross Station in London, finishing this story, that I started in prison.

The man that met me at the door, in the Bahamas was DC George Mason from the National Crime Agency. He and his partner, DC Liz Dawson had traveled to the Bahamas to arrest me for kidnapping and people trafficking. They arrested me and took me, Elena and Ajola to the UK. They brought me back to London, charged me with nine counts of kidnapping and nine counts of people trafficking and, as I pled guilty, the court had leniency on me and sentenced me, to, only 10 years in prison for each count, to run, concurrently. That was almost two hundred years in total! I sat in Pentonville with various cell mates for five years. Not a nice place; locked up twenty three hours per day and eating, really shitty food! I got out six months ago and now I'm on probation and I have to check in with my probation officer, Mandy White, once a week. Like a lot of other ex-offenders, I'm homeless. Life, is back to normal for me! I smell and haven't had a proper wash for over three weeks and food is scarce, to say the least! Like I said, normal! I know, that no one gives a fuck about me!

When I was in prison, I got a letter from Frederick. He told me, that DC Mason, made sure, that Elena and Ajola were safe. They'd done nothing wrong, so he had to let them go and Frederick had sent his private jet to the UK, with two of his guys to pick them up and bring them to Turkey. He'd had to pay a lot of my money to Wilf Sutton and the Albanians, to make sure that the girls and I would remain safe. He said that, he was still investing my money for me. I thought that I must be very rich by now but I had no way to contact him. There was no return address on the letter, he sent to me and under the terms of my probation, I'm not allowed to leave the UK. They have my fake passport, anyway!

All I know, is that he is in Amasya. Maybe, I'll try to find him some day. Elena did not contact me when I was in prison and I have no idea where she is now.

While I was in prison, I heard that Wilf had been killed. Could be, just, jail talk. I don't really give a fuck, if he's alive, or he isn't! Gjin, Sasha and Lorik went to prison, also. Probably still there.

Kylie and Morty disappeared, like all homeless

people do, eventually. No one has any idea where they went. I'm sitting in my box with a blanket around me. It's winter and it's been raining and snowing all morning! I'm so fucking cold, my teeth are chattering! The problem with living in a box, is that, it's never dry or warm!

Suddenly, there's someone banging on the side of my box, "Hey Satch!" My new, next door, box neighbour, an American drug addict by the name of Arnie.

I shake my head; what does he want? "What do you want, Arnie?" Probably needs money – again and I don't have any!

"There's a woman out here, lookin' for you."

"What woman?"

"I don't know, man, a woman!"

I open the flap of the box, thinking, it's probably Mandy White, and go outside. The rain has stopped but it's still cold and cloudy and the wind is blowing. I've still got the blanket wrapped around me.

I see Elena, Ajola and Frederick standing, with big smiles on their faces, next to a big, black limo! Elena's wearing a long, brown fur coat and she looks beautiful! She holds her arms out to me, smiles, takes two steps towards me and says, "Come, Satch, come to me!" Totally surprised, I walk over to her, and she puts her arms around me and says, "I told you, I would love you forever!"

I see Frederick and Ajola smiling at me and he opens the limo door and says, "Come, Satch, let's get you, out of here."

I take Elena's hand and get into the limo. As we drive away, I turn and see, Arnie crawling into my box! Goodbye, London! Hello, tomorrow!

Now, this, really, is the end!

I arrived here, at Frederick's house this morning. I found Frederick and Satch lying on the living room floor. Both of them had been shot in the back of the head and their hands had been cut off. Blood, thick around them. We found Ajola and Elena, upstairs in the bedrooms. Their wrists and ankles were tied to the beds and they had been gutted, slit from their pubic bone to their throats. Their legs were open and they'd, obviously been raped before they were killed. A lot of blood! The place stunk of it! Their intestines were lying beside them. We found 40 kilos of hashish, 700,000 Euros in cash and 10 kilos of cocaine in the kitchen. Whoever did the murders (I suspect it was the Albanians) were not interested in any of that. I am. I found this manuscript and I decided to pass it on to a publisher, in London that I know.

      Wilf Sutton

Printed in Great Britain
by Amazon